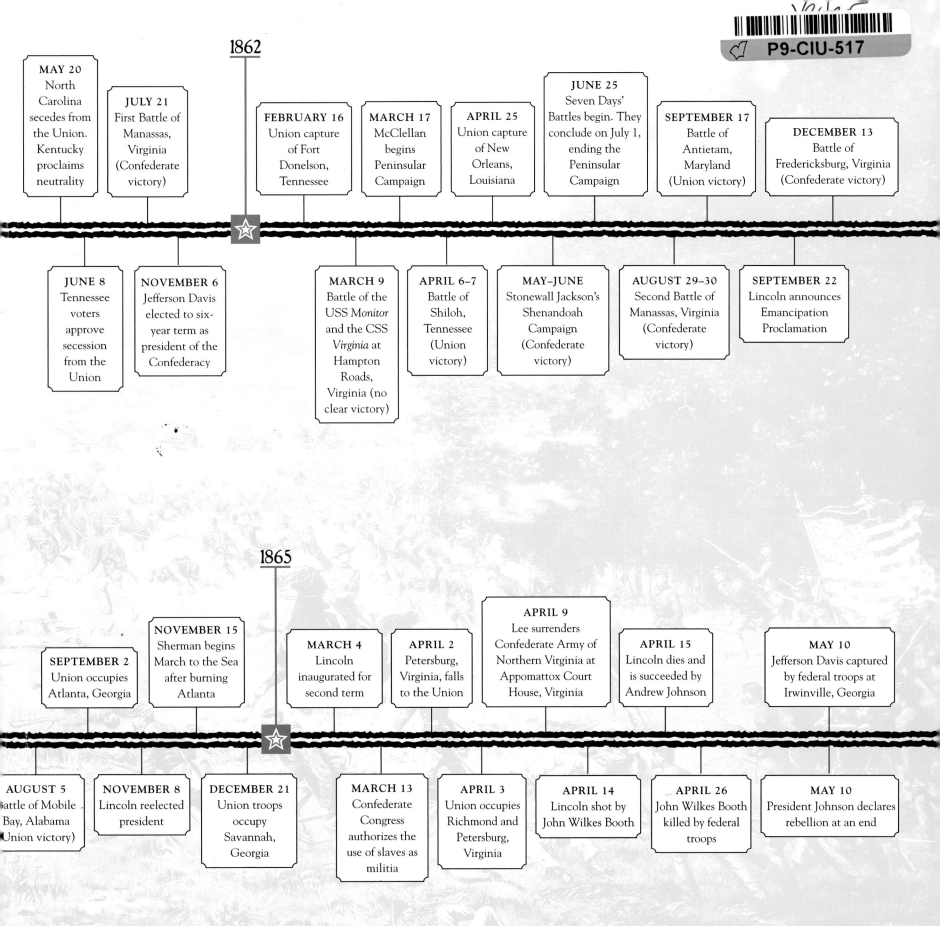

1862

MAY 20 North Carolina secedes from the Union. Kentucky proclaims neutrality

JULY 21 First Battle of Manassas, Virginia (Confederate victory)

FEBRUARY 16 Union capture of Fort Donelson, Tennessee

MARCH 17 McClellan begins Peninsular Campaign

APRIL 25 Union capture of New Orleans, Louisiana

JUNE 25 Seven Days' Battles begin. They conclude on July 1, ending the Peninsular Campaign

SEPTEMBER 17 Battle of Antietam, Maryland (Union victory)

DECEMBER 13 Battle of Fredericksburg, Virginia (Confederate victory)

JUNE 8 Tennessee voters approve secession from the Union

NOVEMBER 6 Jefferson Davis elected to six-year term as president of the Confederacy

MARCH 9 Battle of the USS *Monitor* and the CSS *Virginia* at Hampton Roads, Virginia (no clear victory)

APRIL 6–7 Battle of Shiloh, Tennessee (Union victory)

MAY–JUNE Stonewall Jackson's Shenandoah Campaign (Confederate victory)

AUGUST 29–30 Second Battle of Manassas, Virginia (Confederate victory)

SEPTEMBER 22 Lincoln announces Emancipation Proclamation

1865

SEPTEMBER 2 Union occupies Atlanta, Georgia

NOVEMBER 15 Sherman begins March to the Sea after burning Atlanta

MARCH 4 Lincoln inaugurated for second term

APRIL 2 Petersburg, Virginia, falls to the Union

APRIL 9 Lee surrenders Confederate Army of Northern Virginia at Appomattox Court House, Virginia

APRIL 15 Lincoln dies and is succeeded by Andrew Johnson

MAY 10 Jefferson Davis captured by federal troops at Irwinville, Georgia

AUGUST 5 Battle of Mobile Bay, Alabama (Union victory)

NOVEMBER 8 Lincoln reelected president

DECEMBER 21 Union troops occupy Savannah, Georgia

MARCH 13 Confederate Congress authorizes the use of slaves as militia

APRIL 3 Union occupies Richmond and Petersburg, Virginia

APRIL 14 Lincoln shot by John Wilkes Booth

APRIL 26 John Wilkes Booth killed by federal troops

MAY 10 President Johnson declares rebellion at an end

JAMES M. MCPHERSON

FIELDS OF FURY

☆ THE AMERICAN CIVIL WAR ☆

A Byron Preiss Visual Publications, Inc. Book

ATHENEUM BOOKS FOR YOUNG READERS

NEW YORK LONDON TORONTO SYDNEY SINGAPORE

To Jenny, Jeff, and Gwynne, for the education of the next generation.

Atheneum Books for Young Readers
An imprint of Simon & Schuster Children's Publishing Division
1230 Avenue of the Americas
New York, New York 10020

Text copyright © 2002 by James M. McPherson
All other materials copyright © 2002 by
Byron Preiss Visual Publications, Inc.

*Front jacket photo caption: Fight for the Standard by an unknown artist
courtesy of the Wadsworth Atheneum Museum of Art, Hartford, CT.*
*Title page photo caption: A boy holds Union and Confederate bullets on a
Civil War battlefield in Kentucky.*

The text of this book is set in Goudy.

Printed in the United States of America

10 9 8 7 6 5 4 3 2

Library of Congress Cataloging-in-Publication Data

McPherson, James M.
Fields of fury: the american civil war / written by James M. McPherson.
p.   cm.
"A Byron Preiss Visual Publications, Inc. book."
Includes bibliographic references (p. 93) and index.
Summary: Examines the events and effects of the American Civil War.
ISBN 0-689-84833-1
1. United States—History—Civil War, 1861–1865—Juvenile literature.
2. United States—History—Civil War, 1861–1865—Personal narratives
—Juvenile literature. 3. United States—History—Civil War,
1861–1865—Miscellanea—Juvenile literature. [1. United
States—History—Civil War, 1861–1865.] II. Title.
E468 .M226 2002
973.7—dc21   2001046048

PHOTO CREDITS:
Amistad Foundation Collection / Wadsworth Atheneum: p. 46
Brooklyn Museum of Art: p. 9
Brown University Library: p. 87
Buffalo and Erie County Historical Society: p. 76 (bottom)
Chicago Historical Society: p. 68
Corbis: pp. 50, 75, and 81
Don Troiani Collection: p. 60 (top left)
Franklin D. Roosevelt Library: p. 20
Frank and Marie-Therese Wood Print Collections, Alexandria, VA: p. 33
Galena/Jo Daviess County Historical Society: p. 84
Georgia Historical Society: p. 10 (top)
Gettysburg National Military Park: p. 55
Greenville County Museum of Art: p. 37
Library of Congress: pp. 10 (bottom), 12 (left), 19, 21, 28 (both), 31, 34,
    36, 38 (bottom), 40, 41, 43, 44 (both), 45, 47, 48 (top), 56, 64 (bottom), 66,
    70, 71, 78, 80 (both), 82, 83, 88 (top), and 89
Lloyd Ostendorf Collection: pp. 58 and 59
Minnesota Historical Society: p. 63
Museum of the Confederacy: pp. 14 (top), 17, 51, and 72
Museum of Fine Arts, Boston, MA: p. 53
National Archives: pp. 5, 8, 13, 14 (bottom), 15 (both), 16 (both), 18, 22
    (right), 24, 26 (both), 32, 35, 38 (top), 39, 42, 48 (bottom), 56, 60 (top
    right, bottom), 61, 62, 64 (top), 65, 68 (right), 69 (both), 71, 74, 76
    (top), and 86
New York Historical Society: pp. 11, 12 (right), and 79
Oregon-Jerusalem Historical Society of Ohio, Inc./ The Toledo Soldiers
    Memorial Association: p. 73
Pennsylvania State Archives: p. 88 (bottom)
Smithsonian Institution, NNC, Douglas Mudd: p. 30
State Historical Society of Missouri: p. 29
The Lincoln Museum: p. 52 (bottom)
The Newark Museum/Art Resource: p. 67
U.S. Army Military History Institute: pp. 22 (left) and 52 (top)
West Point Museum Collection, United States Military Academy: pp. 23,
    27, 49, and 85

CONTENTS

The American Civil War was by far the deadliest conflict the United States ever fought. At least 620,000 Union and Confederate soldiers lost their lives in the war. This was almost as many Americans as were killed in *all* the other wars this country has fought, from the Revolutionary War through to the Vietnam War. The Union, border, and Confederate states had a combined population of approximately thirty-two million people in 1861. So the number of soldiers killed in the war was 2 percent of the whole population. If that percentage of Americans was killed in a war fought today, the number of American war dead would be five and a half *million*.

Imagine the impact of such a huge war today and you can get an idea of the effect of the Civil War on the American people 140 years ago. And the war's consequences were much greater in the South, where most of the battles were fought. The war freed the slaves, destroyed the wealth of the plantation owners who had owned most of the slaves, and left many Southern farms, factories, and railroads in ruins. It took nearly a century for the South to fully recover from the war.

Over five generations have now passed since the war, and we are still trying to measure its influence. Many books—by one estimate more than fifty thousand—including *The Red Badge of Courage* by Stephen Crane, *Gone with the Wind* by Margaret Mitchell, and *The Killer Angels* by Michael Shaara, have been written about the Civil War. There are four hundred Civil War "Round Tables" in the United States—groups that meet every month to hear a lecture about the war and discuss its meaning. Millions of people watched the television documentary produced by Ken Burns, *The Civil War*. Millions more have watched such movies as *Gone with the Wind*, *Glory*, and *Gettysburg*. At least forty thousand Civil War enthusiasts dress up in Civil War uniforms and carry weapons just like those used in the war and reenact Civil War battles. Some of the most famous people in American history earned their fame during the Civil War. This group includes Abraham Lincoln, who, as president of the United States, preserved the Union; Jefferson Davis, who was the president of the states that seceded and formed the Confederacy; Ulysses S. Grant, the Union's greatest general; Union general William T. Sherman, whose March to the Sea earned him the undying hatred of the South; and Robert E. Lee, who became a revered legend as the South's greatest general.

The Civil War changed our nation in two important ways. First, it established the identity of the nation as a young, democratic republic that could survive any challenge, even a war between the states. Since 1865, no state has tried to secede, and the United States has remained one nation, indivisible.

Second, the Civil War helped change the laws to give "liberty for all" in the United States. It abolished slavery, which had continued to exist after the American Revolution. By the middle of the nineteenth century, the United States, which boasted of being "the land of the free," had more slaves than any other country. As Abraham Lincoln said in 1854, "The monstrous injustice of slavery . . . deprives our republican example of its just influence in the world—enables the enemies of free institutions, with plausibility, to taunt us as hypocrites."

Above: A Union soldier holding the battle-scarred flag of the 8th Pennsylvania Reserves.

When Lincoln was elected president in 1860 on a platform of preventing the expansion of slavery into any more territories, slave owners feared that his election was the first step toward the eventual abolition of slavery altogether. For this and other reasons, they led their states out of the Union, thereby provoking a war that, in the end, brought about the very event they feared: the end of slavery in the United States.

The soldiers who fought this war knew they were living through an exciting and important time and they wrote a great deal about it in letters home, diaries, and memoirs, many of which were published after the war. *Fields of Fury* quotes from these first-hand accounts. Most soldiers were men, not boys. Their average age was twenty-six. But they often called one another "boys," no matter what their age. And thousands of real boys, seventeen and younger, did serve in the Union and Confederate armies as drummer boys, musicians, and sometimes even as fighting soldiers.

Two of my ancestors fought in the Civil War. Both were from New York State. They represented the age range of most soldiers. My great-grandfather, Luther Osborn, was nineteen years old when he enlisted in the 93rd New York Volunteer Infantry in December 1861. He fought through the rest of the war and lived to the ripe old age of eighty-two. My great-great-grandfather, Jesse Beecher, was a thirty-seven-year-old married man with eight children when he enlisted in the 112th New York Volunteer Infantry in August 1862. He, too, fought through the rest of the war but contracted typhoid fever and died in Wilmington, North Carolina, on April 12, 1865—three days after General Robert E. Lee had surrendered his army at Appomattox. Like three million other Civil War soldiers and sailors, these men endured hardships, danger, suffering, and sickness almost unparalleled in American history. They fought for causes they believed in so deeply that they were willing to sacrifice all—even their lives. I admire them more than I can ever express.

James M. McPherson

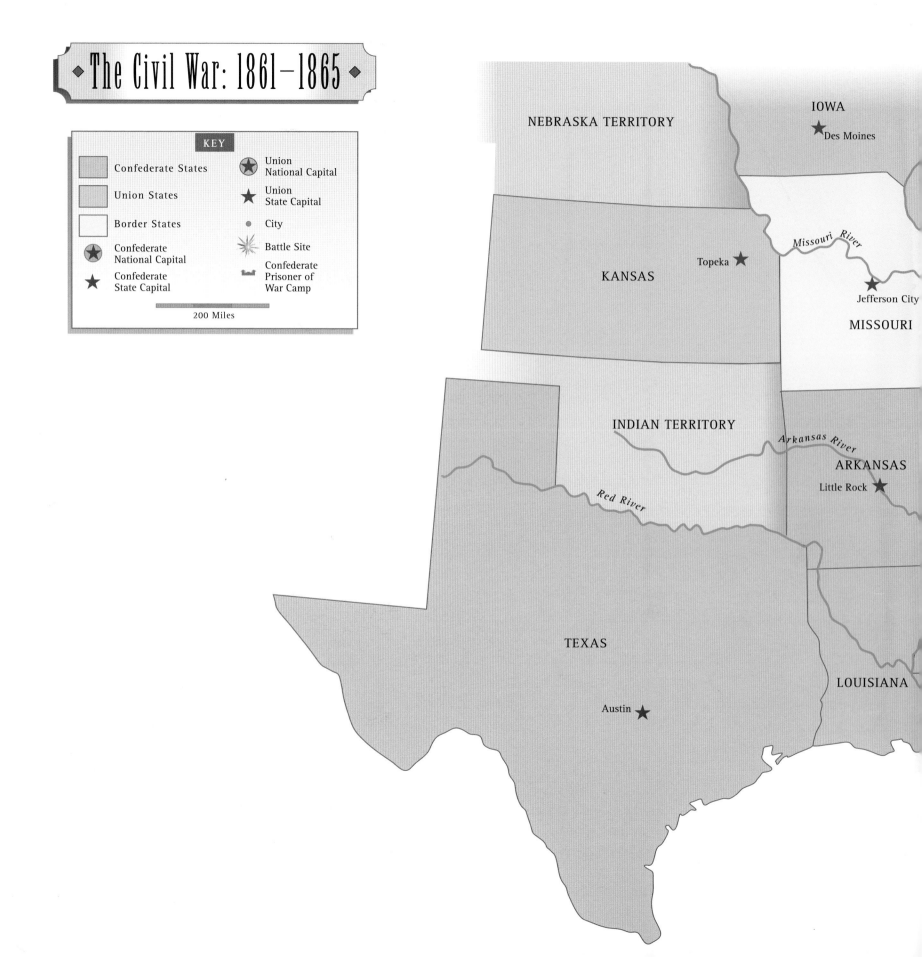

◆ The Civil War: 1861–1865 ◆

KEY

	Confederate States		Union National Capital
	Union States		Union State Capital
	Border States		City
	Confederate National Capital		Battle Site
	Confederate State Capital		Confederate Prisoner of War Camp

200 Miles

NEBRASKA TERRITORY

IOWA

★ Des Moines

Missouri River

KANSAS

Topeka ★

★ Jefferson City

MISSOURI

INDIAN TERRITORY

Arkansas River

ARKANSAS

Little Rock ★

Red River

TEXAS

LOUISIANA

Austin ★

ILLINOIS

INDIANA
Indianapolis

Springfield

OHIO
Columbus

Ohio River

PENNSYLVANIA

NEW JERSEY
Trenton

Harrisburg

GETTYSBURG
July 1–3, 1863

ANTIETAM
September 17, 1862

MARYLAND

Dover

DELAWARE

WEST VIRGINIA
Charleston

Washington, D.C.

Annapolis

Frankfort

KENTUCKY

Richmond

VIRGINIA
(enlarged below)

FORT DONELSON
February 14–16, 1862

Cumberland River

Mississippi River

Nashville

TENNESSEE

CHATTANOOGA
November 23–25, 1863

Raleigh

NORTH CAROLINA

SHILOH
April 6–7, 1862

Tennessee River

CHICKAMAUGA
September 19–20, 1863

Columbia

SOUTH CAROLINA

ATLANTA
July 22, 1864

Milledgeville

Charleston

FORT SUMTER
April 12–14, 1861

MISSISSIPPI

ALABAMA
Montgomery

GEORGIA

MARCH TO THE SEA
November 15–December 21, 1864

Savannah

Jackson

Andersonville

VICKSBURG
April 16–July 4, 1863

aton Rouge

Tallahassee

FLORIDA

MOBILE BAY
August 5, 1864

NEW ORLEANS
April 18–25, 1862

Virginia (enlarged)

OHIO

PENNSYLVANIA

GETTYSBURG
July 1–3, 1863

ANTIETAM
September 17, 1862

Potomac River

MARYLAND

Annapolis

WEST VIRGINIA
(admitted to the Union
June 20, 1863)

FIRST MANASSAS
July 21, 1861

SECOND MANASSAS
August 29–30, 1862

Washington, D.C.

SHENANDOAH CAMPAIGN
May–June 1862

WILDERNESS
May 5–6, 1864

FREDERICKSBURG
December 13, 1862

Charleston

CHANCELLORSVILLE
May 1–4, 1863

SPOTSYLVANIA
May 8–19, 1864

SEVEN DAYS' BATTLES
June 25–July 1, 1862

VIRGINIA

COLD HARBOR
June 1–3, 1864

Richmond

Appomattox
April 9, 1865

PETERSBURG
June 15, 1864
April 2, 1865

PENINSULAR CAMPAIGN
March 17–July 1, 1862

60 Miles

BATTLES OF FIRST AND
SECOND HAMPTON ROADS
March 8–9, 1862

THE ORIGINS OF THE CIVIL WAR

 he Civil War (1861–1865) was the greatest armed struggle on United States soil. There were many reasons why the war started, but the most pressing was slavery. When the United States was still an English colony, slaves were brought from Africa, sold in the South, usually to owners of large farms called "plantations," and put to work. By the time the United States became an independent nation, slavery had become so important to the South's economy that many Southerners believed their way of life could not survive without it.

The stage was already set for conflict as early as 1787, when the newly formed United States drafted its Constitution. This document is the supreme law of the nation, and it set up rules whereby the federal (national) government and individual state governments had certain rights. Slave states would ratify (approve) the Constitution only if it protected slavery. Although some Northerners thought slavery was morally wrong, everyone wanted to work together to make the new nation a success. So the free states agreed to the South's demand, and slavery was protected in the Constitution in Article IV, Section 2, which basically stated that slaves would continue to be the property of their master even when they were in a free state.

As the nation expanded, the slave owners' rights were debated every time people in a territory voted to become a state. The existing states were afraid that if too many new states chose one side or the other, it would upset the balance of government and one group of states would become more powerful than the other. A series of compromises made throughout the early to mid-1800s addressed those differences, but none resolved them. The Missouri Compromise of 1820 brought in Missouri as a slave state but prohibited slavery in any new state north of Missouri's southern border. The Compromise of 1850 brought in California as a free state but included a new Fugitive Slave Act, which made it easier for owners to capture runaway slaves. As time passed, more and more Northerners thought slavery was morally wrong, while most Southerners did not. Unfortunately, each compromise only added to the tension. Then, in 1857, the Supreme Court ruled, in what is known as the Dred Scott decision, that neither the U.S. Congress nor a territory legislature could prohibit slavery in a federal territory. And the situation only got worse.

This hostility became physically violent in the late 1850s in Kansas. The Kansas-Nebraska Act of 1854 gave the residents of Kansas a chance to

Left: The radical abolitionist John Brown. *Opposite*: A detail of Eastman Johnson's painting, *A Ride for Liberty—the Fugitive Slaves,* depicts a slave family escaping on horseback.

Above: The sheet music for "Secession Quick Step."

Above: Several generations of slaves on a plantation.

choose to be a slave state or a free state. People on both sides of the slavery issue rushed from other states to try to influence Kansas voters. These outsiders violently attacked people who didn't agree with them, and the territory quickly turned into a battleground. The territory became known as "Bleeding Kansas" because so many people were killed or wounded. Settlers voted several times on the slavery issue, but reached no decision because each side accused the other of cheating. Kansas remained a territory for the rest of the decade. Not until January 29, 1861, by which time the nation was splitting into two armed camps, did Kansas finally become a free state.

One person who gained infamy during the Kansas crisis was John Brown, an abolitionist (someone who wanted to get rid of slavery). Brown was radical in his ways; he wanted to eliminate slavery any way he could, even if it meant killing people. During the violence in Kansas in 1856, he and some of his followers killed five pro-slavery men. Later, on October 16, 1859, Brown tried to start a slave rebellion. He and some of his followers captured the U.S. arsenal at Harpers Ferry, Virginia. Their plan was to give the guns and ammunition in the arsenal to slaves who would use the weapons to attack their owners. The government's response was swift: Robert E. Lee, a lieutenant colonel at that time, captured Brown and his men two days later. They were tried and convicted, and Brown was executed by hanging. To many, it seemed that the possibility of war was close.

As the nation stood in crisis, it was the presidential election of 1860 that struck the final blow. Abraham Lincoln was elected president in November 1860. Southerners hated Lincoln because they believed he was anti-slavery and intended to eradicate slavery in the South. Before he was even inaugurated in March 1861, seven states, led by South Carolina on December 20, 1860, voted to break away from the United States—to secede—and form their own country. These states—South Carolina, Mississippi, Florida, Alabama, Georgia, Louisiana, and Texas—called themselves the Confederate States of America. They nominated Jefferson Davis as their first president.

In his first inaugural address, Lincoln declared secession the "essence of anarchy." He also said, "no State, upon its own mere motion, can lawfully get out of the Union. . . . They can only do so against law, and by revolution." Lincoln was ready to fight to preserve the Union. The South was ready to fight to preserve its way of life. Their decisions made, the two sides needed only one pivotal event to turn the war of words into a war of bullets. That event would occur soon at Fort Sumter, South Carolina.

Opposite: Plantation slaves at work.

QUICK FACTS

✦ There were approximately 4 million slaves working in the South in 1860.

✦ The importation of slaves was made illegal in the United States in 1808. Although there was some illegal smuggling, the continued growth in the slave economy was primarily caused by population growth among slave families.

✦ Cotton, grown cheaply by slave labor, provided ⅔ of the value of all U.S. exports at the beginning of the Civil War.

✦ In Virginia and South Carolina, freed slaves could be resold into slavery if they did not pay their taxes or had any jail fees or court fines.

✦ *Uncle Tom's Cabin,* written by Harriet Beecher Stowe, was a best-selling novel about slaves suffering under a cruel owner. According to a Beecher family story, when Lincoln met Harriet Beecher Stowe in 1862, he said, "So you're the little woman who wrote the book that made this great war."

Slavery is the ownership of a human being by another. Slaves worked solely for their master, usually without pay, for life. They were property. Children could even be taken from their parents and sold. In addition, slaves could not vote, own land, or travel—not even marriages between slaves were recognized by law.

Many Southerners believed slavery had improved the lives of African Americans. They claimed slavery had civilized African "savages" and provided them with cradle-to-grave security that contrasted favorably with the miserable poverty of the non-slave factory laborer in the industrial North. They said that most slave owners treated their slaves well. People in the North claimed that slaves lived in overcrowded, poorly constructed homes and led lives of unending hard work and cruel treatment—"from day-break to back-break."

The most popular images of slaves are the hardworking cotton-picking field hands and the domestic help of large plantations in the South. In fact, slaves worked everywhere—in small businesses, on the farm, on the ranch, on the docks. Some slaves, such as river pilots and blacksmiths, had skills that made them very valuable. In the cities, some slaves were able to earn money. Although most of it would go to their master, these slaves could keep a portion of their earnings and some used it to buy their freedom. Because slavery was so important to the Southern economy and way of life, many white Southerners would do anything to keep slavery legal—including going to war.

Susie King Taylor was born into slavery in 1848. When Susie was thirteen, she was living with her grandmother in Savannah, Georgia, just before the war began. Shortly after Lincoln's election, news of the Yankees' promises of freedom was widely talked about among the slaves. She recalled the reaction of local whites to this news: "The whites would tell their colored people not to go to the Yankees, for they would harness them to carts and make them pull the carts around, in place of horses. I asked grandmother, one day, if this was true. She replied, 'Certainly not!' that the white people did not want slaves to go over to the Yankees, and told them these things to frighten them."

$100 REWARD!
RANAWAY

From the undersigned, living on Current River, about twelve miles above Doniphan, in Ripley County, Mo., on 2nd of March, 1860, **A NE-GRO MAN,** about 30 years old, weighs about 160 pounds; high forehead, with a scar on it; had on brown pants and coat very much worn, and an old black wool hat; shoes size No. 11.

The above reward will be given to any person who may apprehend this said negro out of the State; and fifty dollars if apprehended in this State outside of Ripley county, or $25 if taken in Ripley county.

APOS TUCKER.

135,000 SETS, 270,000 VOLUMES SOLD.

UNCLE TOM'S CABIN

FOR SALE HERE.

AN EDITION FOR THE MILLION, COMPLETE IN 1 Vol. PRICE 37 1-2 CENTS.
" " IN GERMAN, IN 1 Vol. PRICE 50 CENTS.
" " IN 2 Vols. CLOTH, 6 PLATES, PRICE $1.50.
SUPERB ILLUSTRATED EDITION, IN 1 Vol. WITH 153 ENGRAVINGS,
PRICES FROM $2.50 TO $5.00.

The Greatest Book of the Age.

Far left: A broadside posting a reward for capturing a runaway slave. *Left:* An ad for the book *Uncle Tom's Cabin.* *Opposite:* A slave shows scars from a whipping.

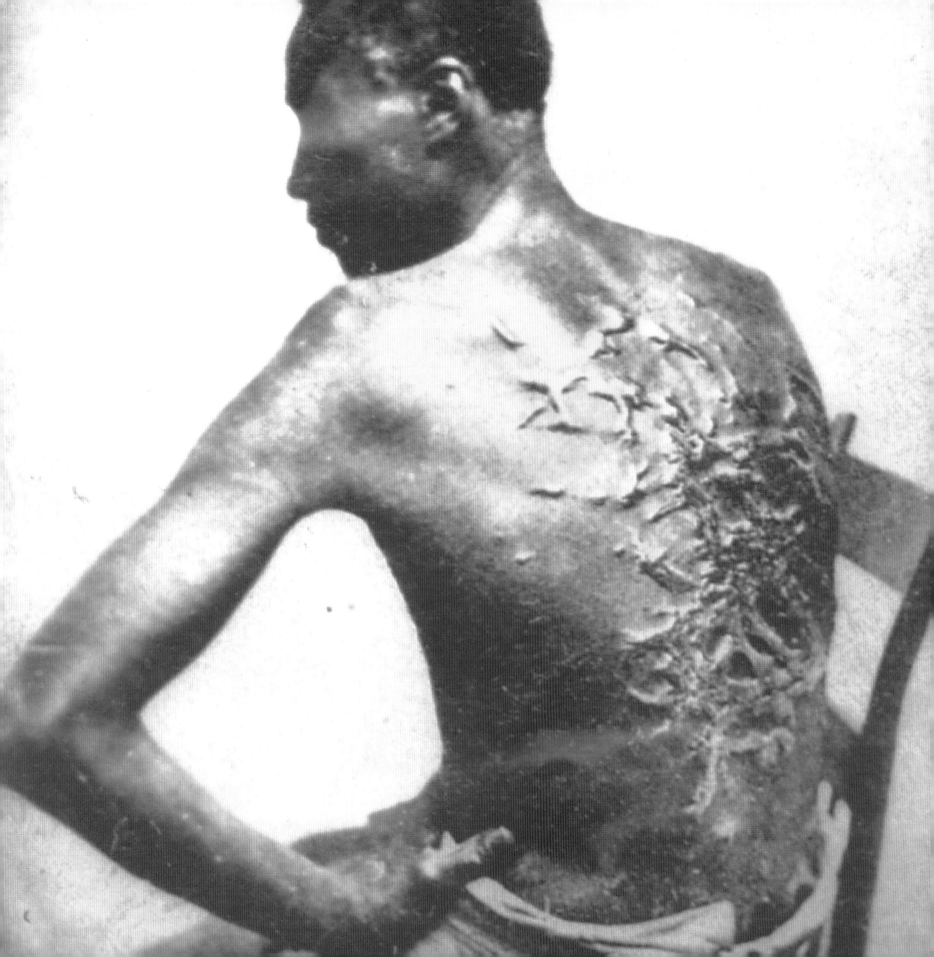

QUICK FACTS

★ Lincoln didn't have a beard until he ran for president in 1860. 11-year-old Grace Bedell wrote him, promising that she would get her brothers to vote for him if he let his beard grow. "You would look a great deal better for your face is so thin," she explained. About a month later, he started growing a beard. After he won the election, he visited Grace and gave her a big kiss.

★ Jefferson Davis was captured by Union forces on May 10, 1865, the same day President Andrew Johnson declared the war was over.

Top: Four of Jefferson Davis's children (from left to right)—Jefferson Jr., Margaret, Varina Anne, and William. *Above:* Abraham Lincoln and his son, Tad. *Opposite left:* Jefferson Davis. *Opposite right:* Abraham Lincoln.

Abraham Lincoln and Jefferson Davis, the two men who would lead their governments during the Civil War, were as different as two men could be. Born in Kentucky on February 12, 1809, Lincoln came from a family of modest means. His parents taught him the value of honesty, hard work, and persistence. His mother died when he was a boy, and he was raised by his stepmother, who encouraged him to study hard. The story of him reading by candlelight after the chores were done is just one of many famous tales about Lincoln. He became a lawyer, then a congressman from Illinois, and finally, president of the United States in 1861. While Lincoln was a lawyer, he met Mary Todd, who was the cousin of one of his law partners. They married in 1842 and had four children: Edward (who died at age four), Robert, Thomas (called Tad), and William, who died in 1862 at the age of eleven from typhoid. During the Civil War, Tad would dress in a lieutenant colonel's uniform and give orders to his father's staff. Robert later became a secretary of war and a U.S. minister to Great Britain.

Lincoln knew how to get along with people. He never let insults or setbacks distract him from his goal of getting the South back into the Union. Lincoln always said that he would do anything and everything—including wage total war—to preserve the Union. Southerners thought he was their greatest enemy. But Lincoln did not seek vengeance against the South. He hoped to heal the scars of the war quickly once the Union won.

Jefferson Davis, also born in Kentucky, on June 3, 1808, was a Mississippi plantation owner when he was made provisional president of the Confederacy, February 18, 1861. He became president of the Confederate States of America on February 22, 1862. Davis graduated from the U.S. Military Academy at West Point and served as a congressman, a senator, and then secretary of war in the cabinet of President Franklin Pierce. Davis originally wanted a military command and only reluctantly accepted the presidency. He married Varina Howell in 1845, and they had six children: Samuel, Jefferson Jr., Margaret, William, Joe, and Varina Anne (called Winnie). Three of the Davis boys died before they became adults.

Proud, arrogant, and convinced of his military expertise, Davis fought almost as much with the people in his own government as the Confederate soldiers did with the Union troops. Jefferson Davis was captured by Union troops in 1865, charged with treason, and thrown in prison. After his release, he wrote a book called *The Rise and Fall of the Confederate Government.* He remained a strong believer in the South and its cause until his death in 1889.

FORT SUMTER

Right: Confederate general Pierre G. T. Beauregard. *Below:* A photo showing the damage at Fort Sumter. *Opposite:* A detail of C. W. Chapman's painting, *The Flag of Sumter.*

In the early spring of 1861, there were seven states in the Confederacy. An editorial in the *Charleston Mercury* declared, "Border southern States will never join us until we have indicated our power to free ourselves. . . . The fate of the southern Confederacy hangs by the ensign halliards of Fort Sumter."

Fort Sumter was located at the entrance to Charleston Harbor. Because Fort Sumter was federal property—belonging to the United States government—it had become a symbol of the North's presence on Southern soil to the new Confederacy. When South Carolina seceded, Governor Francis Pickens ordered that all federal property in the state be given up. Lincoln refused. He sent a messenger to Charleston to inform Governor Pickens that supplies were being shipped to Fort Sumter and that as the ship carrying them did not contain ammunition or weapons, it should be allowed free passage to the fort. The Confederacy's provisional president, Jefferson Davis, saw this as a challenge. He had to make a decision: let Fort Sumter be supplied or capture the fort. On April 9, 1861, the Confederate cabinet agreed with Jefferson Davis. Fort Sumter must be captured before the supply fleet arrived.

Confederate general Pierre G. T. Beauregard ordered his cannons to open fire on Fort Sumter on April 12, at 4:30 A.M. The bombardment continued for two days. Major Robert Anderson, the Union commander of Fort Sumter, was short of ammunition, supplies, and men. There was nothing he could do to keep the Confederates from capturing the fort. He surrendered to Gen. Beauregard on April 14. When news arrived in Washington that the South had fired on Fort Sumter, Lincoln called for volunteers to "repossess the forts . . . which have been seized from the Union." Calling his decision a declaration of war, Virginia and three other states (Arkansas, North Carolina, and Tennessee), also seceded to join the Confederacy. The Civil War had begun.

In Richmond, Virginia, a huge crowd marched to the state Capitol building, lowered the American flag, and ran up the Confederate banner. Everyone "seemed to be perfectly frantic with delight," wrote a participant. "I never in my life witnessed such excitement." An eighteen-year-old student at the University of Virginia in Charlottesville wrote in his diary on April 17, "No studying today. The news of Va.'s secession reached here about 10 oc'lk amid huzzas and shouts. . . . 'War!' 'War!' 'War!' was on placards all about." He was certain the fighting would be over soon because "the scum of the North *cannot* face the chivalric spirit of the South." The first real test for both sides would happen soon, at a creek in Virginia called Bull Run.

QUICK FACTS

⭐ The original Confederate flag (called the "Stars and Bars") looked too much like the Union flag, so Gen. Beauregard designed a new one that arranged 13 stars in an X-pattern. This is the flag that is associated with the Confederacy today.

⭐ The nickname for a Confederate soldier was "Johnny Reb"; for a Union soldier it was "Billy Yank."

⭐ The Confederate "rebel yell" was first used in the 1st Battle of Manassas. It was an eerie, high-pitched scream used to scare federal soldiers. Union soldiers responded with a much deeper "Hurrah!"

⭐ Several Civil War battles have more than one name. Confederates usually named their battles after the town that served as their base of operations. Union forces chose the landmark nearest to the fighting or to their own lines, usually a river or a stream. The 1st Battle of Manassas was called the 1st Battle of Bull Run by the Union.

Left: Union general Irvin McDowell. *Opposite:* Children watch a small group of Union cavalry at Sudley Ford by Bull Run.

The news of the capture of Fort Sumter caused war fever to reach spectacular levels in both the Union and the Confederacy. Both sides thought the war would be over quickly, and nobody wanted to be left out of the fighting. It seemed that everyone was trying to organize a volunteer army unit or trying to join one.

While generals were working hard to turn volunteers into soldiers and supply them with everything needed to fight, people on both sides were demanding swift action. Southerners felt that with another victory, they'd win the war. To many in the North, Richmond, Virginia—the new Confederate capital—was a symbol of power. If the Union could capture Richmond, Northerners thought the Confederacy would collapse. Headlines in Northern newspapers trumpeted ON TO RICHMOND.

Union general Irvin McDowell had another reason to fight. Most of his men were nearing the end of their ninety-day enlistment period. If he waited any longer, his army would literally walk out on him. So he ordered them to march into Virginia. "In gay spirits the army moved forward, the air resounding with the music of the regimental bands and patriotic songs of the soldiers. . . . 'On to Richmond' was echoed and reechoed," wrote federal nurse S. Emma E. Edmonds.

The commander opposing McDowell was the hero of Fort Sumter, Gen. Beauregard. He inspected the positions of troops and fortifications in Virginia. He saw that the Confederate railroad center at Manassas Junction, which connected the important agricultural region of the Shenandoah Valley with the Deep South, was a likely target for Union attack. Beauregard was right. On the morning of July 21, 1861, McDowell launched his assault. It was the first taste of combat for almost everyone—and it showed. Men attacked in groups rather than in lines. Some men accidentally shot their comrades. Others became so excited during the battle that they forgot to fire their rifles; they just kept reloading. But despite their inexperience and confusion, both sides fought well.

Northern reporters, congressmen, and other civilians came to watch the battle and to picnic. From their vantage point two miles away, they could see little but smoke. At first, they thought the Union was winning, and they cheered. But when Confederate reinforcements arrived, the exhausted Union troops were forced to retreat—straight through the shocked picnickers!

The day after the First Battle of Manassas, Lincoln signed a bill for the enlistment of 500,000 men to serve for three years. Three days later, he signed a second bill authorizing another 500,000 men to enlist.

THE ANACONDA PLAN

If there was one man who knew the sorry shape the Union army was in and what it needed to do to fight a successful war, it was its top military commander, General in Chief Winfield Scott. He told President Lincoln that it would take time to turn men into soldiers. He also warned that the war would be long and the fighting hard. While the army was training men, he created a plan designed to keep other countries from sending supplies to the Confederates.

The South did not have enough factories to make its own weapons. But it had something almost as good. It had cotton. In fact, the South was the number one cotton supplier in the world. Great Britain imported three-quarters of its cotton from the South. France and Russia were also big importers of American cotton. This meant that the South had a lot of influence over the governments of these countries. The South could sell the cotton to get weapons and other war supplies. Also, the South could use the enticement of cotton to get Great Britain, France, and Russia to recognize the Confederacy as a new nation. If that happened, then the Confederacy would have allies to help her in the war. Scott was determined to prevent this.

Scott's plan was to send U.S. Navy ships to each of the Confederate ports. When the warships arrived, they would form a blockade to make sure no other ship could get into or out of the port. If any ship refused to stop or turn back, the navy warships would capture or sink it. With no supplies coming in, the Confederates would be "strangled."

Northern newspaper editors laughed at Scott's idea. They made fun of it by calling it the "Anaconda Plan," after the snake that squeezes its victims to death. Many people thought the war would be over long before Scott's plan would have any effect. But Abraham Lincoln liked the idea, and on April 19, 1861, he declared a blockade of the Southern ports.

In the end, it turned out that Scott's Anaconda Plan was a good idea. The blockade lasted throughout the war. Although it took time to make a discernible difference, it did help shorten the war.

Left: D. J. Kennedy's watercolor showing a blockade-runner driven ashore by Union warships. *Opposite*: The "Scott's Great Snake" cartoon illustrated Gen. Scott's Anaconda Plan.

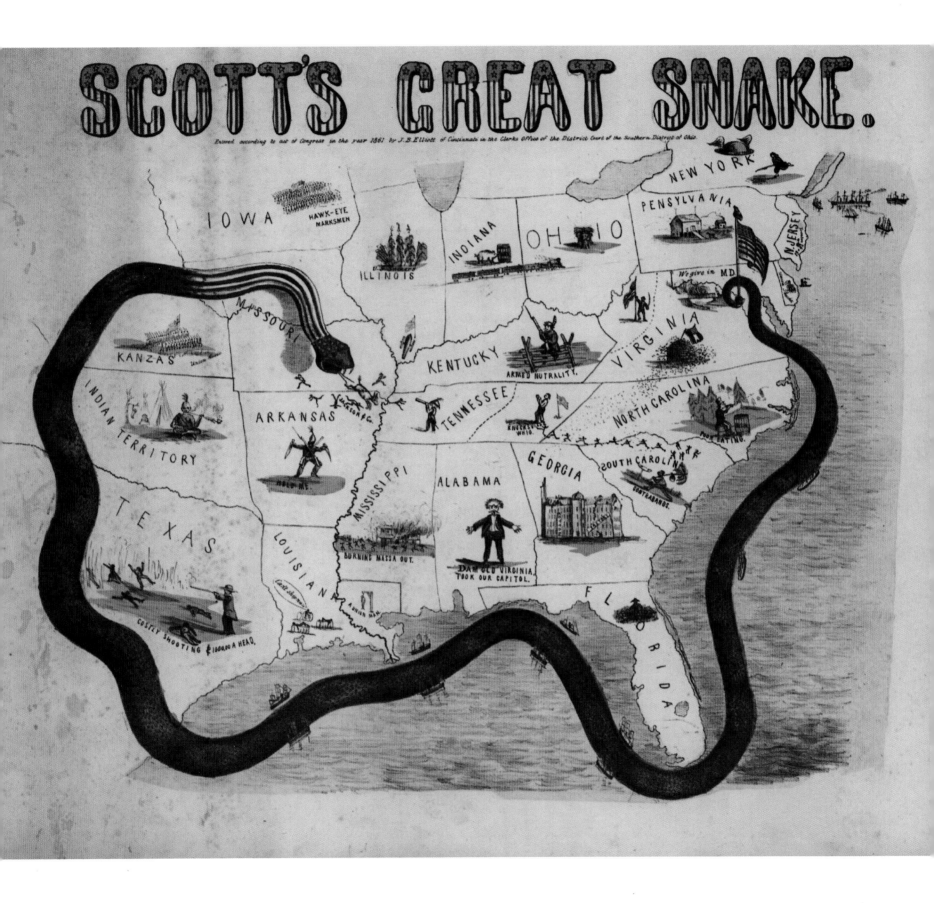

✯ Other border states were Missouri, Maryland, and Delaware.

✯ Samuel Phillips Lee, a relative of Robert E. Lee, chose to remain with the Union. He served in the navy on blockade duty in the Atlantic and on the Mississippi River, and rose to the rank of rear admiral.

✯ Virginians William and James Terrill both became brigadier generals during the war. William fought for the Union and James for the Confederacy. Both were killed in action. Above their graves, the Terrill family placed a single headstone that read: GOD ALONE KNOWS WHICH WAS RIGHT.

✯ Joseph and Willie Breckinridge were brothers from a prominent Kentucky family. Joseph fought for the Union and Willie for the Confederacy during the Battle of Atlanta. When Willie heard that his brother had been captured, he rode all night to where his brother was being held. Willie then gave Joseph some gold coins so he'd have money while a prisoner of war.

Above left: Union general Philip St. George Cooke. *Above right:* Confederate cavalry general James Ewell Brown "Jeb" Stuart. *Opposite:* A detail of H. W. Chaloner's *Cavalry Charge at Yellow Tavern, Virginia, May 11, 1864* depicts the battle where Jeb Stuart was killed.

rom the very beginning, families in the South faced a wrenching conflict, especially in the border states of Kentucky and Tennessee. They became examples of how the war tore apart families. Although both were slave states, many people in each state believed slavery was wrong. While Tennessee officially joined the Confederacy, many citizens, including Senator Andrew Johnson, chose to remain with the Union. Kentucky tried to remain neutral, but neutrality was impossible. The desperate seesaw campaigns that ravaged these two states made this truly a brothers' war, for Kentucky and Tennessee were the states with the most men on both sides of the slavery issue. Where should their loyalties lie? Those who chose loyalty to the country over that to the state or to family often found themselves regarded as traitors.

This family dividing conflict touched people at the highest levels of army and government. Shortly after the war started, Jeb Stuart, who would become a famous Confederate cavalry leader, wrote to his wife, Flora: "I am extremely anxious about your Pa and your brother. . . . How can they serve Lincoln's diabolical government?" Stuart's father-in-law, Philip St. George Cooke, a Virginian like Stuart, chose to remain in the Union army. Stuart's brother-in-law, John Rogers Cooke, left the Union infantry to join the Confederacy. The senior Cooke thus found himself fighting both his son and his son-in-law. On at least two occasions, Stuart and St. George Cooke fought on the same battlefield.

Commander Charles Steedman returned to America after a voyage abroad in 1861 to discover that his home state, South Carolina, had seceded. Though many Southerners serving in the military would have resigned their commissions and joined the Confederacy, Steedman announced his loyalty to the Union. When his brother, James, heard the news, he wrote to Charles, "I felt that my blood was cold in my veins . . . my Brother a Traitor to his Mother Country. . . . " How could "a Brother in whose veins flows the same blood, Southern, *true* Southern . . . ever allow Northern principles to contaminate his pure soul?" Charles wrote in reply, "I am as I have always been, a Union man— I know no North or South . . . all that I know is my duty to flag & country."

When the war ended, too often family members who had fought on opposing sides would never see or speak to each other again. In the case of Philip St. George Cooke and his son, John, years would pass before they reconciled. (Stuart died in May 1864 at the Battle of Yellow Tavern in Virginia.)

FORT DONELSON

QUICK FACTS

★ Just before the war, Confederate general Floyd had been U.S. Secretary of War and had allegedly transferred weapons to Southern arsenals.

★ Buckner's son, Simon Bolivar Buckner Jr., would become a famous general in World War II.

★ Soldiers in the Civil War described their experience in combat with the slang expression "seeing the elephant." "Elephant" was the word soldiers used to describe combat, large or small. "Seeing the elephant" meant going into battle.

★ In 1862, Union troops were given new, small tents to replace the bulky large tents they had been using. Because they had to crawl into these tents like dogs, the troops called them "dog tents." Today those tents are called "pup tents."

Above: C. W. Reed's painting of Gen. Grant on horseback.

ort Donelson was an important Confederate fort on the Cumberland River near the Kentucky-Tennessee border. The Union attack on Fort Donelson in February 1862 was led by Ulysses S. Grant, at the time a little-known brigadier general with a poor reputation. However, Grant's troops had recently captured nearby Fort Henry on the Tennessee River. If Grant succeeded in capturing Fort Donelson, the route to northern Alabama would be wide open for the Union troops.

On February 14, Grant ordered navy commander Flag Officer Andrew H. Foote to take his small fleet of six gunboats and attack the riverside of the fort while his troops surrounded the fort on land. Even though the Confederate artillery succeeded in damaging the fleet and wounding Foote, Grant won the first round of fighting by surrounding the fort on its landward side.

That night, the commander of the Confederate defenders, General John Floyd, held a meeting with his two subordinate commanders, Brigadier General Gideon Pillow and Brigadier General Simon Bolivar Buckner. They discussed their three choices: surrender now, wait and hope that help would come before they were forced by starvation to surrender, or attempt a breakout—to fight their way out. Floyd decided to attempt a breakout. They quickly left to get their troops into position.

The night of February 14 was bitterly cold, and a howling snowstorm made troop movement difficult. But thanks to the storm, the Union sentries couldn't see what the Confederates were doing. The rebel attack was launched just after dawn on the frosty morning of February 15. The desperate Confederate troops pushed the Union soldiers back almost a mile. But just when the Confederate troops were about to complete the breakout, they retreated. Their generals were afraid that even if they succeeded, their exhausted troops would be destroyed by a Union counterattack. The next day, the Confederates surrendered to Grant.

Fort Donelson was the first major Union victory in the war. It was a big success for Grant, too. Lincoln promoted him to major general, and because Grant used the words "unconditional surrender" in his demand to the Confederate defenders, he became famous as "Unconditional Surrender" Grant.

The defeat was a terrible blow to the Confederacy. The Deep South was now open to direct attack by the Union troops.

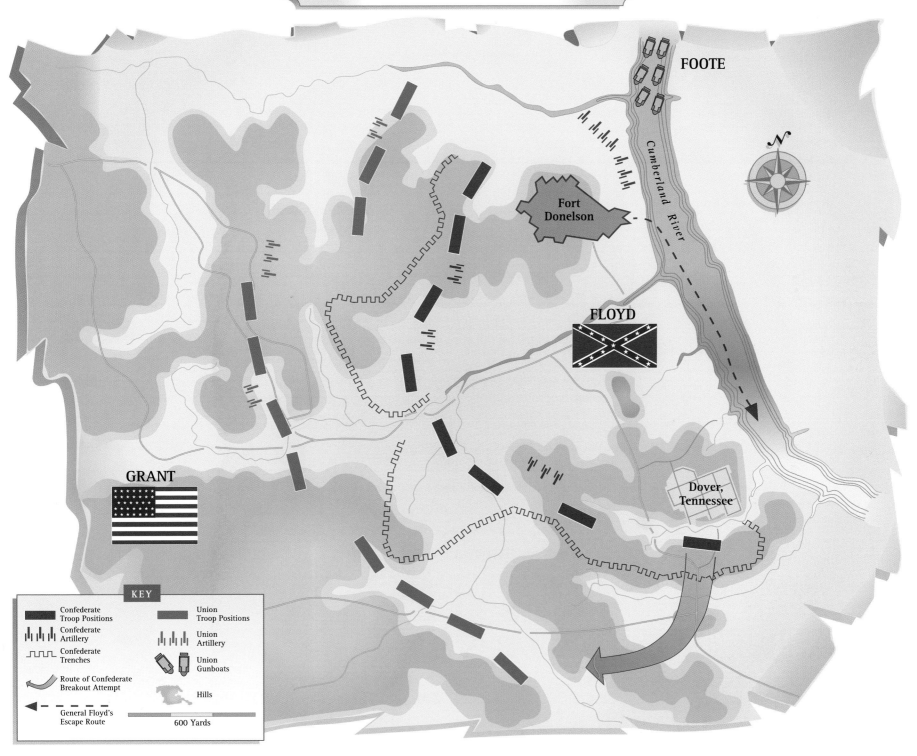

Fort Donelson Campaign: February 1862

FOOTE

Cumberland River

Fort Donelson

FLOYD

GRANT

Dover, Tennessee

KEY

Confederate Troop Positions

Union Troop Positions

Confederate Artillery

Union Artillery

Confederate Trenches

Union Gunboats

Route of Confederate Breakout Attempt

Hills

General Floyd's Escape Route

600 Yards

QUICK FACTS

★ The *Monitor* had to be towed from Brooklyn to Hampton Roads because it was so slow.

★ The *Virginia* and the *Monitor* never fought each other again. The *Virginia* was destroyed by the Confederates when the federals captured Norfolk in May 1862. A storm off Cape Hatteras, North Carolina, sunk the *Monitor* on the last day of 1862.

★ The Confederates tried to build many more ironclads after the success of the *Virginia,* but they completed only 22 of them because materials were scarce. The Union built some 58 monitors and several other experimental ironclads.

★ The Union cannon was called the "Dahlgren gun," after its developer, Admiral John A. Dahlgren. It was nicknamed the "Soda-Water Bottle" because of its strange, bottlelike shape.

Top: A gun squad loading a cannon onto a monitor's deck. *Above:* The crew and mascot on the deck of the Union monitor USS *Onondaga.*

Naval history was made off the coast of Virginia in the spring of 1862. The two battles of Hampton Roads signaled the end of the era of the wooden ship and the beginning of a new era of ships covered in iron.

The two ironclads that caused this revolution in naval warfare were the homeliest vessels afloat. The Confederate *Virginia* (known in history by its original name *Merrimack*) looked like a barn floating on the water. The Union *Monitor* looked like a raft with a giant hockey puck on it. Both boats had such weak engines that they could barely move. Their decks were so close to the surface of the water that waves could easily splash over them. Despite all their faults, they were more effective in battle than any other ships in the world.

The First Battle of Hampton Roads took place on March 8, 1862. The Confederates' plan was to have their new ironclad, CSS *Virginia*, sail out of Norfolk and attack and destroy the nearby Union blockade fleet of wooden steamships. The Union ships fired shot after shot, but the cannonballs and shells were, as one federal observer said, "having no more effect than peas from a pop-gun." When Union cannon shells struck the *Virginia*, the noise inside the ironclad was deafening, but the crewmen kept to their posts. The rebel ship steamed toward its first target, the big wooden warship USS *Cumberland*. *Virginia* had attached to its bow a large ram. *Virginia* smashed its ram into the side of the *Cumberland*, tearing a seven-foot hole into its hull, sinking it.

Its ram wrenched off by the collision with the *Cumberland*, the *Virginia* could only use its cannons against its next challenger, USS *Congress*, and the two ships shot repeatedly at each other. Fires broke out on the *Congress*, and the Union warship exploded when the fires reached its stores of gunpowder. The *Virginia* then attacked the USS *Minnesota* and damaged it. When night came, the *Virginia* returned to Norfolk, intending to finish off the blockade fleet the next day. It would have, except that on March 9, when *Virginia* sailed out to attack the wooden fleet, it found the Union ironclad *Monitor* waiting for it. It had just arrived from its port in Brooklyn, New York.

The Second Battle of Hampton Roads was the first battle between two ironclads. For hours, they steamed around each other, firing constantly and often at close range. But as with *Virginia* the previous day, the cannonballs and shells just bounced off their sides. Finally, the exhausted crews sailed their ships away from each other. Both sides claimed victory.

Opposite: The *Virginia* sinks the *Cumberland* in the painting *First Battle of Hampton Roads* by H. Harrison.

The Battle of Shiloh was the next big test for Major General Grant—and he almost failed. Grant's usual military strategem was to plan what he would do to the enemy, not to worry about what the enemy would try to do to him. Grant was planning for his next big battle, which he intended to happen at Corinth, Mississippi. But on April 6, 1862, Grant and his men were at Pittsburg Landing near Shiloh Church in Tennessee when the Confederates, led by General Albert Sidney Johnston, surprised him.

The fighting at Shiloh reached a savage level never before encountered in the war. One of Grant's subordinates, General William T. Sherman, worked hard to rally the troops and get them to stand and fight. But for thousands of untested Union soldiers, the shock of combat was too much. They fled to the rear. Fortunately, thousands of Southern boys also ran from the front with terror in their eyes. Even so, at the end of the day on April 6, it appeared as if the Confederates had won the battle. That evening, they spent the night in the Union camps they had captured.

When some of Grant's frightened officers advised a retreat before the rebels could renew their assault in the morning, he replied: "Retreat? No. I propose to attack at daylight and whip them." That's exactly what he did the next day, April 7. By midafternoon, the relentless Union advance had pressed the rebels back to the point of their original attack. In the end, it was the rebels who abandoned the Union camps and retreated in defeat. The Union troops, too tired after all the hard fighting to pursue the enemy over muddy roads, flopped down in exhaustion in their recaptured camps.

Before Shiloh, Grant had believed that one more Union victory would end the rebellion. Now he "gave up all idea of saving the Union except by complete conquest." Shiloh launched the country into the flood tide of total war.

Fifteen-year-old Elisha Stockwell Jr. from Wisconsin fought at Shiloh. As his unit advanced to fight the rebels, he later wrote, "The first dead man we saw was . . . leaning back against a big tree as if asleep, but his intestines were all over his legs and several times their natural size. I didn't look at him the second time as it made me deathly sick."

Above left: Johnny Clem, a drummer in the 22nd Michigan Infantry, who became famous as "Johnny Shiloh." *Above right:* Union troops defend themselves against attack.
Opposite: Members of the 21st Missouri volunteers show their weapons.

★ To help pay for the war, the U.S. Congress passed the first national income tax on August 2, 1861. The income tax ended in 1872. People who made more than $800 per year had to pay the tax. It was not until the 16th Amendment was ratified in 1913 that Congress obtained the power to establish an ongoing income tax.

★ To make the hundreds of thousands of uniforms needed, textile manufacturers in the North created a compressed woolen fabric called "shoddy." Because the fabric rapidly fell apart, the word "shoddy" soon came to mean anything poorly made.

★ Just before the war started in 1861, salt cost $2 per pound in the South; by 1862, its price had reached $60 per pound in some places. The cost had inflated 3,000 percent.

★ Both governments also collected money by charging a tax on imported goods. This tax was called a "duty."

★ "Graybacks"— Confederate paper money —were so named because the poor paper and ink used often caused the paper money to turn gray after being circulated.

Above: A Confederate $500 bill with a portrait of General "Stonewall" Jackson in the lower right-hand corner. *Opposite:* A U.S. Army supply depot.

Mary Chesnut of Richmond, Virginia, wrote in her diary on August 25, 1861: "Honorable Clayton, assistant secretary of state, says we spend two millions a week. Where is all that money to come from? They don't want us to plant cotton but to make provisions. Now, cotton always means money—or did, when there was an outlet for it, anybody to buy it. Where is money to come from?"

Where indeed? Wars are expensive. Armies need weapons—and clothes, food, wagons, tents, and thousands of other things. The U.S. Congress calculated in 1863 that the war was costing the Union $2.5 million a *day*.

Back then, "real" money was gold or silver coins, or paper money that said on it that it could be exchanged for a stated amount of gold or silver. For instance, if you had a five-dollar bill that had the words "Gold Certificate" or "Silver Certificate" on it, you could trade it in for five dollars' worth of gold or silver. But in 1862, because gold and silver were in such short supply, the Union created "greenbacks"—paper money that was legal but that couldn't be exchanged for gold or silver. This is the sort of money we use now. But in the 1860s, paper money was a newfangled idea that didn't sit well with people. Because it was backed by people's faith in the federal government, the value of the greenbacks went up and down throughout the war, depending on how well the Union was doing on the battlefield. No one knew exactly what they were worth.

At the start of the war, cotton amounted to more than half of all U.S. exports. Since cotton was grown only in the South, the Confederacy seemed in pretty good shape to pay for everything it needed. But it also wanted other countries, especially Great Britain and France, to agree that the Confederacy was an independent nation. This agreement is called "diplomatic recognition." At first, the South refused to sell cotton unless it was granted recognition. It didn't work. Britain already had enough cotton to last for months. By the time it was gone, Britain had found other sources of cotton. And when the South decided to sell cotton overseas again, its ships encountered the Anaconda Plan with its blockade of Confederate ports. It became difficult, sometimes even impossible, for blockade-runners to leave Southern ports with cotton, sail to ports in Great Britain or France, and return with guns or ammunition.

The financial situation kept getting worse and worse for the Confederacy. Soon it, too, had to print paper money. But if people in the North were suspicious of the value of their greenbacks, people in the South had even less faith in Confederate money. They had good reason. By the end of the war, Confederate money wasn't worth the paper it was printed on.

Above: A photo of David Farragut after becoming an admiral. *Opposite:* An engraving showing the Union fleet fighting between Fort Jackson and Fort St. Philip.

New Orleans, located near the mouth of the Mississippi River, was the largest city in the Confederacy. It was also a major port. If the Union could capture New Orleans, it could cut off a huge amount of supplies that the South needed to fight the war. The only way the Union forces could capture the city was by sailing up the Mississippi River. But two strong forts, Fort Jackson, on the west bank, and Fort St. Philip, on the east, guarded that approach. The rebels had also strung a thick chain, supported by anchored boats, across the river from one fort to the other. Many felt that attacking those forts was suicide.

But Union flag officer David Glasgow Farragut was not afraid of the forts. To his wife he wrote: "I have now attained what I have been looking for all my life—a flag [command of a fleet]—and having attained it, all that is necessary to complete the scene is a victory." If he couldn't destroy the forts, he'd simply find a way to break the chain and steam past them. And that's just what he did.

The attack on the forts began on April 18, 1862. For six days, Union ships shelled the forts in an attempt to destroy them. It didn't work. On the night of April 23–24, two Union ships sailed up to the chain. Even though the ships were fired upon, they managed to make a break in the chain. At 2:00 A.M. on April 24, seventeen of Farragut's warships steamed upriver.

Rebel response was immediate and total. The forts and the small rebel fleet immediately opened fire. Civilian boat captains deliberately sunk their ships in the Union fleet's path. Farther upriver, Confederate tugboats pushed fire rafts filled with flaming pine and pitch into the current to float down to the Yankee ships. All this happened in a space of less than one square mile. It must have been the greatest fireworks display in American history.

Despite everything, Farragut's fleet fought its way through. As the Union fleet steamed up to the city the next day, George Washington Cable later recalled that "the crowds on the levee howled and screamed with rage. The [sailors on the Union ships] answered never a word; but one old tar (sailor) on the *Hartford,* standing . . . beside a great pivot-gun, so plain to view that you could see him smile, silently patted its big black breach and . . . grinned." When the mayor of New Orleans refused to surrender, Farragut ordered a unit of marines to enter the city and raise the U.S. flag over the public buildings.

Shortly after the fall of the city, Sarah Morgan of Louisiana angrily wrote in her diary, "This is a dreadful war to make even the hearts of women so bitter! . . . *I* talk of killing [Yankees] for what else do I wear a pistol and carving knife?"

THE PENINSULAR CAMPAIGN

QUICK FACTS

⭐ Gen. Lee was known affectionately as "Marse Robert" by his men. "Marse" was the slave slang word for "master."

⭐ Gen. McClellan's troops loved him and called him "Little Mac." He was also called "Young Napoleon."

⭐ The Union often named its armies after rivers in the areas where they fought. The Army of the Potomac fought mostly in eastern Virginia. The Army of the Shenandoah originally fought mostly in western Virginia. The Army of the Cumberland fought in Tennessee and the West. The Confederacy usually named its armies after states: Lee's was named the Army of Northern Virginia.

⭐ Gen. Joseph Hooker, who later became a commander of the Army of the Potomac, got his nickname "Fighting Joe" Hooker during the Peninsular Campaign.

Above: Union officers resting in camp. George Armstrong Custer, who would later become famous fighting Indians in the West, is lying beside the dog. *Opposite:* Union mortars were used to shell Confederate defenses during the Peninsular Campaign.

Shortly before Farragut captured New Orleans, the new commander of the Army of the Potomac, General George McClellan, made a plan to capture the Confederate capital of Richmond, Virginia. He would launch his Peninsular Campaign in March 1862, attacking Richmond from the south, advancing up the Virginia peninsula between the James and York Rivers. McClellan took 110,000 men—and the Union hope of swift, war-winning victory—with him.

General Robert E. Lee was the military adviser to President Jefferson Davis. When Lee saw what McClellan was doing, he created a plan to stop him. The Confederate troops facing McClellan were led by General Joseph E. Johnston. When McClellan's men landed near Yorktown, Virginia, in early April, Confederate General John Bankhead Magruder was ordered to delay the federal troops to give the Confederates time to construct defenses around Richmond and to bring in reinforcements. Magruder cleverly ordered his small force, hidden behind hastily built fortifications, to stage a "show" for the enemy. His troops marched back and forth. Soldiers shouted orders to ghost units. His men made so much noise and kicked up so much dust that it sounded as if a huge army was getting ready for battle. The trick worked. McClellan, convinced the rebel troops outnumbered his, refused to move until *he* was reinforced. McClellan did not attack Yorktown for a month. When he did, in early May, his troops discovered that the Confederate forces had left.

At first, the Union attack up the peninsula went well, and they advanced toward the Confederate capital. Then, at the Battle of Seven Pines, also known as Fair Oaks, Johnston's reinforced army stopped McClellan less than ten miles from Richmond. The battle lasted two days, from May 31 to June 1, 1862. Johnston was wounded, and President Davis selected Robert E. Lee as Johnston's replacement. McClellan was overjoyed when he heard the news. He considered Lee "likely to be timid and irresolute in action." But time would soon reveal which general was timid and which was bold.

To assess the threat he was facing, Lee ordered his flamboyant cavalry commander, James Ewell Brown "Jeb" Stuart, to ride behind McClellan's lines and find out everything he could about the Army of the Potomac. On June 12, Stuart and 1,200 men took off on what turned out to be one of the most spectacular escapades of the war. They wound up making a complete circuit around the Union rear. By the time his ride was over, Stuart had not only gathered all the information Lee needed, he had also made a fool of the Union cavalry and become a great hero of the South.

QUICK FACTS

✶ Stonewall Jackson and his sister, Laura, were orphans who loved each other deeply. But the Civil War drove them apart. Jackson joined, and became a hero of, the Confederacy. Laura, however, was a staunch Unionist who was disgusted over her brother's decision. They never reconciled.

✶ Jackson's men captured a lot of supplies during the campaign. According to his calculations, the goods seized were worth $125,185.

✶ Winchester, Virginia, located in the Shenandoah Valley, was captured and recaptured 76 times during the war.

✶ Brigadier General Jackson got his immortal nickname "Stonewall" during the 1st Battle of Manassas. When Confederate brigadier general Barnard E. Bee saw Jackson solidly keeping his position and not running away from the attacking Yankees, he shouted, "There stands Jackson like a stone wall!"

Lee needed to make sure that McClellan, still threatening Richmond, would not be reinforced. He decided to create a diversion, using some of his men to make Lincoln and the other Union leaders think he was attacking Washington, D.C., with a large army. If Lee was successful, McClellan would not get the reinforcements he was demanding. Lee needed a bold and brilliant general to make his bluff work. That general was Thomas J. "Stonewall" Jackson. The place where Lee decided Jackson would stage the bluff was the strategically important Shenandoah Valley of Virginia.

Called the "breadbasket of the Confederacy," the valley's rich farmland was a major source of food. Also, the valley was like a gigantic highway protected by the Allegheny Mountains to the west and the Blue Ridge Mountains to the east. Confederate troops marching down the valley threatened the North, especially Washington, D.C.

In a series of stunning moves in May to June 1862, Jackson's "foot cavalry" moved up and down Virginia's Shenandoah Valley, fighting first one Union division, then another. When it was all over, Jackson's small army of 17,000 men had fought and won five battles. More important, Lee's bluff had worked. Jackson's campaign had diverted 60,000 Union soldiers from other tasks and disrupted two major strategic movements: the campaign in east Tennessee and the attempt to reinforce McClellan.

After one particularly bloody battle, one of Jackson's subordinates, Colonel John Patton, felt sorry for all the dead enemy soldiers he saw. "Colonel," Jackson asked, "why do you say that you saw those Federals fall with regret?" Patton said that they were very brave in battle and that it seemed such a shame that brave men had to die. Jackson replied: "Kill them all. I do not wish them to be brave."

Military experts ever since have studied Jackson's Shenandoah Campaign and have written lengthy papers explaining Jackson's success. But it was best said by one rebel private who wrote, "General Jackson 'got the drop' on them in the start, and kept it."

Left: Confederate general Thomas J. "Stonewall" Jackson. *Opposite:* A detail of D. E. Henderson's painting, *Halt of the Stonewall Brigade,* depicts Gen. Jackson surrounded by his men.

THE SEVEN DAYS' BATTLES

Right: Union general George B. McClellan and his wife, Ellen. *Below:* Alfred R. Waud's drawing, *Battle of Friday on the Chickahominy,* shows part of the battle at Gaines' Mill.

In June 1862, McClellan's Peninsular Campaign had stalled. Even though the Army of the Potomac was less than ten miles away from the Confederate capital, McClellan refused to order an attack on Richmond. When he was asked why he was not advancing, he wrote to his superiors in Washington, "The rebel force is stated at 200,000 . . . I shall have to contend against vastly superior odds. . . . If [the Army of the Potomac] is destroyed by overwhelming numbers . . . the responsibility cannot be thrown on my shoulders; it must rest where it belongs." So much for Robert E. Lee being the cautious and hesitant general!

Although Lee had the psychological advantage over McClellan, Little Mac still had 110,000 very real men under his command. Even with reinforcements, Lee was still outnumbered, having only about 90,000—the largest army he would ever command. But Lee saw that the advantage lay with him, and he was going to seize it with both hands—with a bold plan to capture the Army of the Potomac and win the war for the South with one blow.

Lee launched his attack against the Army of the Potomac's positions east of Richmond on June 25. For the next seven days, Lee's army fought the retreating McClellan and his men. The back-to-back battles in Oak Grove, Mechanicsville, Gaines' Mill, Garnett's and Golding's Farms, Savage's Station, Frayser's Farm, and finally Malvern Hill came to be known as the Seven Days' Battles. In the end, the Army of the Potomac escaped destruction by retreating to its base on the James River at Harrison's Landing, Virginia. From there, the army withdrew from the peninsula. Despite his retreat, McClellan claimed that he had won because he had saved the Army of the Potomac. Lincoln, however, knew that Robert E. Lee was the real victor. If he was going to defeat the Army of Northern Virginia, he'd have to find himself another general.

Even though there was a lot of fighting during the Seven Days' Battles, soldiers discovered that most of their time in the army was spent doing things *other* than fighting. Connecticut infantryman James Sawyer wrote about a typical camp life schedule in his regiment: "We have to get up at 5, breakfast at 6. Then comes cleaning the tents and washing dishes. At 7 if on guard we go on duty if not, drill from 7 to 9 A.M. Then it takes us from 9 to 11 to scour our guns and equipment. At 11, drill until 1 P.M., when dinner is ready. Drill again from 2 to 3. At 4½ comes dress parade. Then supper. And by that time it is dark. Lights are put out at 9½."

Opposite: Union private Emory Eugene Kingin (note that he is not dressed in a regular uniform)—at Gaines' Mill.

THE SECOND BATTLE OF MANASSAS

Above: Two men sit near the ruins of a railroad bridge at the battlefield. *Opposite:* A Union officer leads a charge on the Confederate positions.

After the Peninsular Campaign, President Lincoln decided that he needed a new general to fight against Robert E. Lee in Virginia. His choice was General John Pope, a successful officer from the western theater. But Pope proved to be a terrible commander. In his first address to his new troops, he insulted them. Many felt he had called them cowards. Then, when he moved his army into Virginia, he treated the civilians very harshly. When Lee heard what Pope was doing, he said that he would take care of "that miscreant Pope." It was on the battlefield of Manassas, by the Bull Run River, exactly where the Union had suffered defeat in 1861, that Pope met disaster and humiliation in 1862.

The Second Battle of Manassas displayed the bold strategy of Robert E. Lee and its brilliant execution by Stonewall Jackson. Lee split his command between his subordinates, Stonewall Jackson and James Longstreet. Pope was fooled into sending his 60,000 soldiers to attack Jackson's 20,000 troops on August 29, 1862. By the end of the day, Pope had convinced himself that he had Jackson on the ropes. The next day, Pope renewed the attack with everything he had. Jackson's situation was desperate. At one point, wrote Lieutenant Robert Healy of the 55th Virginia, "We received urgent orders to reinforce a portion of our line . . . which was about to give way. . . . The troops occupying this place had expended their ammunition and were defending themselves with rocks . . . which many were collecting and others were throwing."

But Jackson had a backup plan. He sent a courier to Lee, requesting reinforcements. That was the message Lee was waiting for. The very moment when Pope was convinced he was about to win, Lee signaled Longstreet and sprang his trap. Longstreet rapidly moved up a battery of cannons onto a rise overlooking the Union's left flank and gave the order to fire. The Union troops staggered under one volley after another. Then Longstreet's fresh troops charged. It was like 1861 all over again.

The Union lines wavered, then broke. The rebels kept up the attack. On September 1, at Chantilly, just twenty miles from Washington, D.C., the Union troops put up a vicious defense. Lee attempted a final attack during a drenching thunderstorm. When his offensive was beaten back, Lee retreated with his exhausted troops.

Again a Union commanding general had failed his troops. Pope's defeat at the Second Battle of Manassas was so great that Lincoln immediately relieved him of command and restored McClellan to the post.

QUICK FACTS

★ Union Pvt. Johnny Cook, a 15-year-old-bugler with Battery B, 4th U.S., received a Medal of Honor for his actions at Antietam.

★ There were over 23,000 casualties at Antietam, almost 4 times the total suffered by American soldiers on the Normandy beaches on D-Day in World War II.

★ A future president fought at the Battle of Antietam: Sgt. William McKinley of the 23rd Ohio.

★ At one point in the battle, Confederate brigade commander John B. Gordon came upon an elderly man and his son lying side by side on the ground. Gordon wrote, "The son was dead, the father mortally wounded. The gray-haired hero called me and said, 'Here we are. My boy is dead, and I shall go soon. But it is all right.'" Gordon himself was wounded 3 times in the battle.

★ Clara Barton was one of the few nurses who went out onto the battlefield as the fight was raging. As she was taking care of a wounded soldier, a bullet passed under her arm and struck the man, killing him.

Above: President Lincoln (center) meets with Major General John A. McClernand (left) and detective Allan Pinkerton (right), who helped gather information on the rebels. *Opposite:* Confederate soldiers killed at Bloody Lane.

Up until September 1862, the Confederacy had been fighting a defensive war. There had been defeats in the West, including Fort Donelson and New Orleans. But overall, this strategy seemed to be working because of the Army of Northern Virginia's important victories in Virginia. Now Gen. Robert E. Lee felt the time was right to change the defensive strategy into an offensive strategy. He wanted to invade the North, attacking through Maryland into Pennsylvania. A successful invasion might finally prod Great Britain and France into recognizing Confederate nationhood and also convince some Northerners to demand an end to the war. The stakes were high. If Lee miscalculated and lost, his army might be destroyed and, with it, the Confederacy. But President Davis agreed that it was a risk worth taking.

Lee marched his army into Maryland in September 1862. But in a field near the town of Frederick, two Union soldiers found a copy of Lee's battle plans, wrapped around three cigars lost by a careless Southern officer. When Gen. George McClellan, again commander of the Army of the Potomac, received the documents, he said, "Here is a paper with which, if I cannot whip Bobbie Lee, I will be willing to go home!" But he moved slowly, thereby giving Lee a chance to prepare to meet the Union troops. The battle was finally joined on September 17 near the town of Sharpsburg, by Antietam Creek. Lee's troops, with their backs to the river, were facing an enemy almost twice their number.

McClellan attacked all day long, inflicting and receiving terrible casualties. The Battle of Antietam, called the Battle of Sharpsburg by the Confederates, was the bloodiest day of fighting in the Civil War. No one knows exactly how many men were killed or wounded, but it has been estimated that nearly 6,000 men lost their lives and another 17,000 were wounded. But at the end of the day, Lee's army still clung to most of its positions.

Although Lee's army was badly bloodied and in a precarious position, he kept them on the battlefield the next day, September 18, almost as if to dare McClellan to launch another attack. McClellan refused. That evening Lee ordered his army to return to Virginia.

Because Lee's invasion was stopped, Antietam was a strategic success for the Union. More important, Great Britain and France refused to give diplomatic recognition to the South. The victory also gave President Lincoln the ammunition he needed to make an important announcement—the Emancipation Proclamation.

QUICK FACTS

⭐ Poet Ralph Waldo Emerson wrote the poem "Boston Hymn" to commemorate the Emancipation Proclamation.

⭐ The Emancipation Proclamation officially allowed African Americans to enlist in the armed services.

⭐ Congress passed a law in 1862 that freed the slaves in the District of Columbia.

⭐ Prior to the Emancipation Proclamation, slaves who had escaped from the South, called "contrabands," were used only as laborers by the Union armies. After it, however, escaped slaves could become soldiers.

Top: The Emancipation Proclamation.
Above: Frederick Douglass. *Opposite:* An African-American family crossing Union lines.

President Lincoln had been planning to announce his Emancipation Proclamation, in which he declared his intention to free slaves in the rebel states, for some time. Members of his cabinet urged him to wait until after the Union had won a victory on the battlefield. They believed that because of the many defeats the Union armies had suffered, announcing the Emancipation Proclamation without a battlefield victory to back it up would be judged an act of desperation.

On September 22, 1862, five days after the Battle of Antietam, Lincoln called his cabinet into session and said, "I think the time has come. I wish it were a better time. I wish that we were in a better condition." Nevertheless, Antietam was a victory, and Lincoln intended to warn the rebel states that unless they returned to the Union by January 1, 1863, their slaves "shall be then, thenceforward, and forever free."

Lincoln's enemies mocked his Proclamation. They pointed out that it did not free the slaves in the border states that belonged to the Union, and since rebel states had seceded, the Proclamation could not be enforced there.

But Lincoln knew that by issuing the Proclamation, he had changed the way the war would be waged. After January 1, the Proclamation would turn Union forces into armies of liberation—if they could win the war. It also invited the slaves to help them win it. The abolitionist Frederick Douglass understood what Lincoln had done, writing, "We shout for joy that we live to record this righteous decree."

Even though almost all slaves in the South were illiterate, word of the Emancipation Proclamation eventually reached slaves throughout the Confederacy. When they heard about the Proclamation, many made their way to Union lines. Ultimately, almost 200,000 former slaves fought in Union armies.

The dismissive attitude in the South regarding the Emancipation Proclamation was reflected by Sarah Morgan, who lived in Baton Rouge, Louisiana. She wrote in her diary on November 9, "If Lincoln could spend the grinding season on a plantation, he would recall his proclamation. As it is, he has only proved himself a fool, without injuring us."

But the former slave Susie King Taylor recalled that January 1, 1863, "was a glorious day for us all, and we enjoyed every minute of it, and as a fitting close and the crowning event of this occasion we had a grand barbecue."

QUICK FACTS

★ The most famous African-American unit in the war was the 54th Massachusetts. Their story was made into the movie *Glory*.

★ Frederick Douglass had two sons who served in the 54th Massachusetts.

★ Most officers of black regiments were white men. The highest-ranking African-American officers in the Civil War were Union majors Francis E. Dumas and Martin R. Delany.

★ An estimated 10,000–12,000 African-American sailors served in the U.S. Navy during the Civil War. Approximately 179,000 served in the U.S. Army.

★ The Medal of Honor was created by the U.S. Congress in December 1861.

★ Robert Blake, an escaped slave, served on the gun crew of the USS *Marblehead*. In a battle against the Confederate shore batteries near Charleston, South Carolina, he received the Medal of Honor for his heroism. Blake was the first African American to receive this new award.

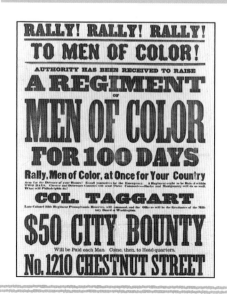

RALLY! RALLY! RALLY!
TO MEN OF COLOR!
AUTHORITY HAS BEEN RECEIVED TO RAISE
A REGIMENT
OF
MEN OF COLOR
FOR 100 DAYS
Rally, Men of Color, at Once for Your Country

Arm for the Defence of your Homes! Enroll yourselves for the Emergency. A Regiment ought to be Raised within TWO DAYS. Chester and Delaware Counties will send Three Companies—Bucks and Montgomery will do as well. What will Philadelphia do?

COL. TAGGART
Late Colonel 12th Regiment Pennsylvania Reserves, will receive, and the Officers will be the Graduates of the Military Board at Washington.

$50 CITY BOUNTY
Will be Paid each Man. Come, then, to Head-quarters,
No. 1210 CHESTNUT STREET

As early as the outbreak of the war, African Americans in the North had tried to enlist in the Union army, but they were denied. One such frustrated volunteer was Jacob Dodson, who wrote to Union Secretary of War Simon Cameron, "I desire to inform you that I know of some 300 reliable colored free citizens of this city who desire to enter the service for the defense of the city [Washington, D.C.]. . . . I have been three times across the Rocky Mountains in the service of the country with Frémont and others."

But their desire to fight under arms would not be fulfilled until after Lincoln issued the Emancipation Proclamation on January 1, 1863. The new African-American units fought bravely, even when outnumbered or when confronted with overwhelming rifle and cannon fire.

The reason for their determination was expressed by Joseph E. Williams, an African American from Pennsylvania who helped recruit freed slaves: "I will draw my sword against my oppressor and the oppressors of my race. I must avenge my debasement. I will ask no quarter, nor will I give any. With me there is but one question, which is life or death. And I will sacrifice everything in order to save the gift of freedom for my race."

The Union's use of African-American troops enraged the Confederates. The Confederate Congress authorized that all captured African-American soldiers, as well as any of their white commanding officers, be put to death. Any captured African-American soldier who was not killed was sold into slavery. Knowing the fate that awaited them if they were captured by the Confederates, African-American soldiers fought with a fierceness and conviction unmatched by their white brethren in blue.

A naval officer whose ship was being repaired at the Union base in Beaufort, North Carolina, observed a black regiment under the command of James Beecher, brother of Harriet Beecher Stowe: "There is a firmness & determination in their looks & in the way in which they handle a musket that I like," he wrote to his wife. "It looks like fight & Port Hudson has proved that they will do so. I never [would] have believed that a common plantation [N]egro could be brought to face a white man. I supposed that everything in the shape and spirit & self respect has been crushed out of them generations back, but am glad to find myself mistaken."

Left: A poster calling for African-American men to enlist in the Union army.
Opposite: A group of African-American guards from the 107th United States Colored Troops.

Top: A unit of ten- and twelve-year-old musicians from the 93rd New York Infantry. *Above:* Union general Ambrose E. Burnside. *Opposite:* Union troops wait in the trenches at Fredericksburg.

The Army of the Potomac welcomed a new commander on November 7, 1862. He was Ambrose E. Burnside, a general who had successfully invaded North Carolina and who had served under McClellan at Antietam. Twice before, Burnside had been offered command of the Army of the Potomac, and both times he had refused, saying that he felt he was not qualified for the top command. This time, Lincoln ordered Burnside to assume command. As the Battle of Fredericksburg would tragically prove, Burnside was right. He never should have been made commander.

Burnside's original plan to capture Richmond was sound. He planned to use pontoon bridges to cross the Rappahannock River at Fredericksburg, Virginia, and march south to capture Richmond before Lee could shift his forces north to stop him. But the pontoons Burnside needed were delayed for a week. By the time Burnside got them, Lee had discovered Burnside's plan and had moved his men into position, digging in along the hills south of the Rappahannock.

When he saw what Lee had done, Burnside decided that "the enemy will be more surprised by a crossing immediately in our front." Lee *was* surprised, because it was the worst decision a general could make. Lee's men were positioned along four miles of high ground overlooking Fredericksburg. Union troops would have to charge over a half mile of open fields.

On December 13, Burnside ordered his men to attack the Confederate positions on a steep hill named Marye's Heights. The result, as one subordinate predicted, was "murder, not warfare." As Gen. James Longstreet's artillery commander, Edward Porter Alexander, said, "A chicken could not live on that field when we open on it." Funneled by ravines, a marsh, and a drainage ditch toward a sunken road that was fronted by a half-mile-long stone fence at the base of the hill, the advancing Union troops were slaughtered by the waiting Confederate defenders. When night fell and the temperature plunged, wounded men trapped on the battlefield froze to death. Burnside's aides convinced him to order a retreat. Once again, a newly appointed commander of the Army of the Potomac had confronted Lee on the field of battle and failed.

Captain William T. Lusk later wrote in a letter home: "Gone are the proud hopes . . . [The army] has strong limbs to march and meet the foe, stout arms to strike heavy blows, brave hearts to dare—but the brains, the brains! have we no brains to use the arms and limbs and eager hearts with cunning?"

QUICK FACTS

⭐ Gen. Hooker created insignia badges for each corps to instill unit pride. It was the first time such badges were used in an American army, which are still used today.

⭐ When asked why he had frozen the way he did at Chancellorsville, Hooker said, with extraordinary honesty, "Well, to tell the truth, I just lost confidence in Joe Hooker."

⭐ The telegraph, a new system of electronic communication that transmitted coded messages over copper wire, was widely used for the first time for military purposes during the Civil War. President Lincoln used the system to stay in close contact with his generals all across the country.

Above: Jackson's attack on the right wing of the Union army at Chancellorsville. *Opposite:* E. B. D. Julio's painting, *The Last Meeting of Lee and Jackson.*

His name was Fighting Joe Hooker. He was the new commander of the Army of the Potomac. It was news that gladdened the hearts of his troops, for the men knew him and liked him. Over the winter, Hooker quickly worked to restore the morale of the Army of the Potomac, which was so low that two hundred men a day were deserting.

Hooker launched his campaign in late April 1863. He boasted, "My plans are perfect, and when I start to carry them out, may God have mercy on General Lee, for I will have none."

Lee was still entrenched at Fredericksburg. Hooker commanded 130,000 men; Lee commanded 60,000. Hooker's plan was to keep part of his army in front of Lee's Army of Northern Virginia. The other part would cross the Rappahannock far upstream and head south to cut off Lee's supply lines. Hooker's troops managed to reach Chancellorsville, Virginia, nine miles west of Fredericksburg. The Army of Northern Virginia was caught between two forces. For once, it appeared that a Union general had outfoxed Lee. Hooker assumed that, after fighting started on May 1, Lee would have to retreat.

Instead, Lee decided to attack. After conferring with Stonewall Jackson, Lee grasped the initiative and from May 2–4, 1863, Lee repeatedly maneuvered his forces in such a way as to give them superiority or equality of numbers at every point of attack. Like a rabbit mesmerized by a gray fox, Hooker was frozen into immobility and did not use half his power at any time in the battle. At its end, a thoroughly demoralized and defeated Hooker ordered a retreat.

Chancellorsville was Robert E. Lee's greatest victory. But there was little cheering in the Confederate camp. The battle had cost the Army of Northern Virginia 13,000 casualties, just under one-fourth of its total forces. The greatest loss was the man Lee called his "strong right arm." Stonewall Jackson had been shot and wounded by his own men by mistake. A week later, complications had set in and Jackson was dead.

Sue M. Chancellor, whose family had founded Chancellorsville, recalled her experience of the battle: "Oh, the horror of that day! There were piles of legs and arms outside of the sitting room window and rows and rows of dead bodies covered with canvas. . . . If anybody thinks that a battle is an orderly attack of rows of men, I can tell him differently, for I have been there. . . . The woods around the house were a sheet of fire; the air was filled with shot and shell; horses were running, rearing, and screaming."

The Union was suffering defeat after defeat in Virginia. The campaign in the West, however, was a different story. There the Union plan to seize control of the Mississippi River was succeeding. By the fall of 1862, Vicksburg was the last major strong point on the Mississippi River still in Confederate hands. Situated on a high bluff overlooking the river and defended by the Army of the Mississippi under John C. Pemberton, its combination of natural and man-made defenses was formidable. If the Union was going to split the Confederacy in two and isolate Arkansas, Texas, and Louisiana, it had to take Vicksburg.

Almost immediately after Grant began his advance on April 16, 1863, his men ran into trouble. The Confederate cavalry commander, General Nathan Bedford Forrest, destroyed Grant's long and poorly defended supply lines. Grant had to retreat and rethink what he would do next.

He decided that the best way was to isolate, then lay siege to, the city. In a seventeen-day campaign during which his army marched 180 miles and fought and won five engagements against separate enemy forces, Grant eliminated any chance of outside help for Vicksburg. He then closed off a now demoralized enemy behind the Vicksburg fortifications. The siege began on May 18, 1863. Grant would wait out the rebels, using cannons and mortars to shell the city. The streets became too dangerous to use. Civilians dug caves in the bluff and lived in them during the siege. Food shortages forced people to eat anything they could find. Horses, mules, dogs, cats, and even rats and mice wound up in family cooking pots.

Sieges are basically long waiting periods. With lots of time on their hands, soldiers on both sides actually socialized and discovered that they had a lot in common. Fifteen-year-old Union soldier Elisha Stockwell recalled that on "moonlight nights [rebels] used to agree to have a talk, and both sides would get up on the breastworks and blackguard each other and laugh and sing songs for an hour at a time, then get down and commence shooting again."

Finally, on July 4, 1863, the Confederates surrendered. A day earlier, in the small crossroads town of Gettysburg, Pennsylvania, another great battle had also ended. These events marked the turning point in the war.

Top left: Confederate general John C. Pemberton. *Bottom left:* A drawing depicting life in a cave during the siege of Vicksburg. *Opposite:* A detail of a painting by an unknown artist portrays a Union attack at Vicksburg.

★ The Battle of Gettysburg saw the largest concentration of Confederate artillery: 150 guns. The ear-splitting roar was heard as far away as Pittsburgh, 160 miles away.

★ At one point in the battle, Gen. John B. Gordon heard a bullet strike Confederate general Ewell. "Are you hurt, sir?" Gordon asked. "No, no," replied Ewell. "I'm not hurt. . . . It don't hurt a bit to be shot in a wooden leg."

★ Because of the slow way Meade pursued Lee, Lincoln said that the pursuit reminded him of "an old woman trying to shoo her geese across a creek."

★ Gen. Abner Doubleday's men took up a defensive position on Gettysburg's cemetery—Cemetery Ridge. The sign on the arched gateway to the cemetery read: ALL PERSONS FOUND USING FIREARMS IN THESE GROUNDS WILL BE PROSECUTED WITH THE UTMOST RIGOR OF THE LAW.

★ Bayard Wilkeson, a 19-year-old Union lieutenant, almost had his right leg severed by artillery fire. He used his sash to make a tourniquet, then he amputated the shattered limb with his pocketknife. Despite his efforts, he did not survive.

★ The Battle of Gettysburg had the highest number of casualties in the war, with a total of 51,112. The Union suffered 23,049 casualties and the Confederates suffered 28,063.

In June 1863, Robert E. Lee launched his second invasion of the North. Some of his men wore tattered uniforms—or no uniforms at all. Almost all were poorly fed. But after two years of hard fighting, the Army of Northern Virginia had established itself as one of the greatest armies of all time. Once again, Lee divided his army and gave his corps commanders—Gen. James Longstreet, Gen. Richard Ewell, and Gen. A. P. Hill—much freedom of action. Once again, he ordered his "eyes and ears"—Jeb Stuart and his cavalry—to scout ahead and keep him informed of the location of the Army of the Potomac. Unfortunately for Lee, Jeb Stuart chose to gather the information by doing the same thing he did a year ago during McClellan's Peninsular Campaign. Stuart attempted another "Grand Rounds" around the Army of the Potomac. This time, Stuart found himself fighting a series of battles that drove him farther and farther from Lee. The result was that, for seven days, Lee did not know the position of either Stuart *or* the enemy.

In the meantime, President Lincoln had become unhappy with Gen. Hooker. On June 28, 1863, Lincoln replaced him with Major General George Gordon Meade. He did this in the nick of time—three days later, the Army of the Potomac would find itself in the middle of one of the greatest engagements in the Civil War.

Gettysburg was a battle that began without either commanding general near the field. It was at a place where neither had intended to fight. But independently of their intentions, it was here that a battle destined to become the largest and most important of the war was fought. It began on July 1, when Confederate general Hill decided to have his corps drive a small Union cavalry force out of the small, redbrick crossroads town of Gettysburg so they could get supplies. The first day of the battle was led by subordinate commanders. The fighting was confused, as both sides fought for superior position. Lee and Meade, upon hearing of the struggle, rushed forces to the town.

When the second day dawned, it appeared that the Confederates had an overwhelming advantage. But they lost precious time getting their men, especially Gen. Longstreet's corps, into position. It was not until late afternoon that Longstreet was able to launch his attack.

Gen. Meade had the time he needed—just barely—to get reinforcements in place. At the end of the day, the heights of Big Round Top, Little Round

Opposite: A detail from Paul Philippoteaux's cyclorama of the Battle of Gettysburg.

Above: A Confederate sniper killed at Gettysburg.

Above: Confederate general George Pickett.

Top, and Cemetery Ridge remained in Union hands. Still, the Confederates held the important location known as the Peach Orchard and a small part of Culp's Hill.

On the third day, Lee decided that he was going to attack the middle section of the Union defenses. The man he ordered to lead the charge and smash through the Union line was General George Pickett.

Gettysburg native Jennie McCreary later wrote of the third day, "All felt that *this* day must decide who should conquer. . . . [That afternoon] the cannonading began . . . such cannonading no one ever heard. Nothing can be compared to it, one who has never heard it cannot form any idea how terrible it is."

What Jennie McCreary heard was the artillery fire announcing the most famous assault in the war, Pickett's Charge. After an exchange of artillery fire, at 1:45 P.M. the rebel soldiers, stretched out along a front almost a mile wide, marched across an open field toward the enemy. When they got within 1,200 yards of the Yankee lines, the Union cannon opened fire, followed by the rifles and muskets of the troops. Wave after wave of men fell. Some members of Pickett's command succeeded in penetrating the federal first line of defense. But it was a doomed effort. The attack had been shattered. Over half of the attackers had fallen. When the survivors returned to their lines, a shaken Lee apologized, saying, "It's all my fault. It is I who have lost this fight, and you must help me out of it the best way you can. All good men must rally."

The next day, July 4, the battlefield was quiet. Both sides were too tired to attack. That night, the Army of Northern Virginia, wounded and weary, headed south in retreat. Meade pursued, but he was too cautious to press his advantage. The Army of Northern Virginia escaped across the Potomac River on July 14.

Four months later, on November 19, 1863, President Lincoln attended a ceremony dedicating a national cemetery at Gettysburg. Lincoln began his speech with the sentence "Fourscore and seven years ago our fathers brought forth on this continent a new nation, conceived in liberty and dedicated to the proposition that all men are created equal." Two minutes and less than three hundred words later, he had explained to his audience that the best way to honor the men who had died on the battlefield was to continue to fight the war. That speech, the Gettysburg Address, has become one of the most famous speeches in history.

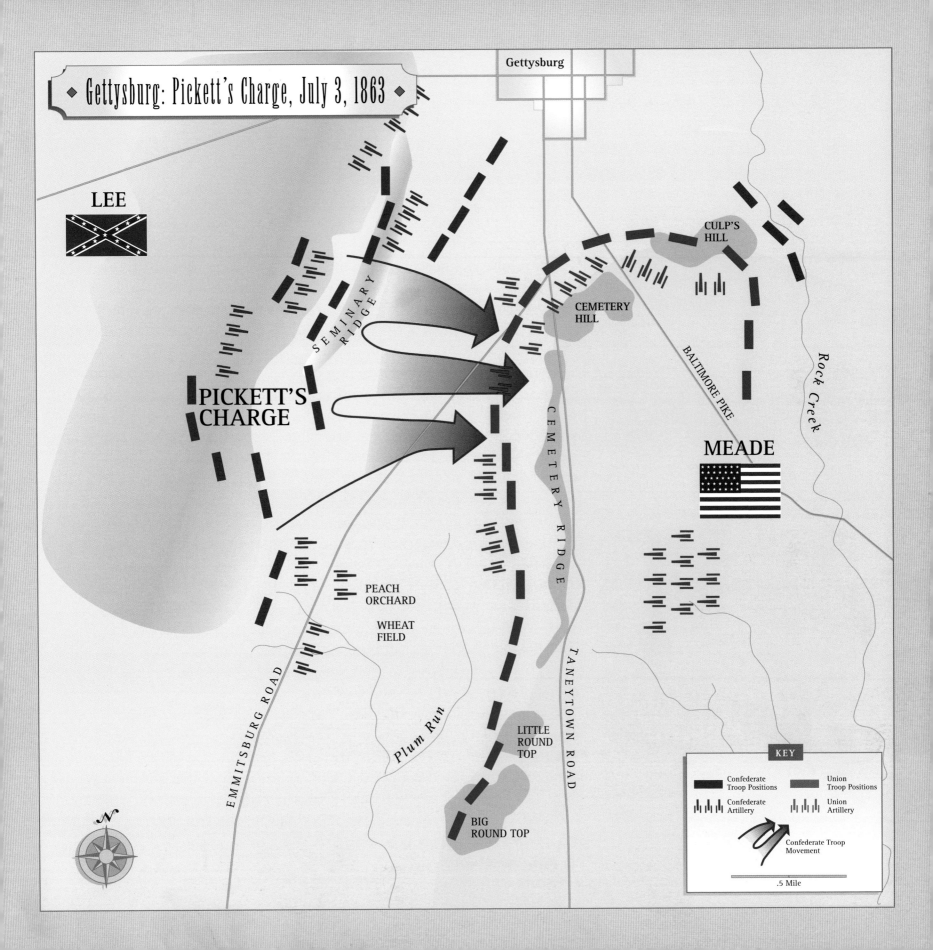

Gettysburg: Pickett's Charge, July 3, 1863

Gettysburg

LEE

PICKETT'S CHARGE

MEADE

SEMINARY RIDGE

CEMETERY HILL

CULP'S HILL

CEMETERY RIDGE

BALTIMORE PIKE

Rock Creek

PEACH ORCHARD

WHEAT FIELD

EMMITSBURG ROAD

Plum Run

TANEYTOWN ROAD

LITTLE ROUND TOP

BIG ROUND TOP

N

KEY

Confederate Troop Positions

Union Troop Positions

Confederate Artillery

Union Artillery

Confederate Troop Movement

.5 Mile

QUICK FACTS

✦ It has been estimated that as many as 400 women disguised themselves as men and fought as soldiers on both sides during the war.

✦ Some women who followed their husbands to battle were adopted as mascots and became known as "Daughters of the Regiment."

✦ Many soldiers were not old enough to shave, so it was easy for a woman to disguise herself as a man. She cut her hair short, deepened her voice, and wore men's clothing. Because recruiting inspections did not include a physical examination, women were able to pass without their identities being discovered.

Above: A group of women from Philadelphia sew a Union battle flag. *Opposite:* Pauline Cushman, a Union spy, in uniform.

In the 1800s, a woman's world was the home and family. The war dramatically changed this. With so many men in uniform, women had to join the workforce. Women were employed in occupations ranging from government civil service to agricultural fieldwork and manufacturing.

But women also made contributions to the war closer to the battlefields. Many served as nurses taking care of sick and wounded soldiers. And a number of women were spies.

Emma Edmonds was a highly skilled spy for the North. She was a master of disguise, successfully assuming various identities: that of a white Southern man named Charles Mayberry and using silver nitrate to darken her face, that of both an African-American man and woman. She even fooled some Yankee soldiers into thinking she was a private by the name of Franklin Thompson.

The South, too, had its share of female spies. One of the most successful was Rose O'Neal Greenhow, a Washington, D.C., socialite widow in her forties. Though her Southern sympathies were well known, that did not stop many high-level politicians from attending her parties. Her combination of beauty and charm made her irresistible to men of power and to those who wanted to appear powerful. She was quite frank about her efforts to wheedle information from her admirers. "I employed every capacity with which God has endowed me, and the result was far more successful than my hopes could have flattered me to expect," she wrote in her autobiography.

Even after she was caught and sent to prison, Greenhow managed to send important information to the South. Paroled and sent back to the South in 1862, she later went to Europe and served as an unofficial ambassador for the Confederacy. She attempted to return to the Confederacy in October 1864. The ship she was on was stopped near Wilmington, North Carolina, by a Union blockade. Greenhow tried to slip past the blockade in a rowboat but when the rowboat capsized, she drowned.

The most sensational thing some women did was disguise themselves as men and fight on the front lines. One woman who did this was Loreta Janeta Velazquez, who fought for the Confederacy as a soldier. Disguised as Lieutenant Harry T. Buford, she fought at the First Battle of Manassas, at Fort Donelson, and the Battle of Corinth, in Mississippi, where she was wounded. She would continue her fight both on the battlefield as a soldier and behind Union lines as a spy. After the war, she published a memoir of her incredible exploits.

CARING FOR THE WOUNDED

QUICK FACTS

☆ Dr. Mary Walker was awarded the Medal of Honor for her work in the Civil War. She was the only woman to receive the award. In 1917, a military review commission took away her medal because she had not participated in combat. It was restored to her on June 10, 1977.

☆ Out of all the surgeries performed in the Civil War, 3 out of 4 were amputations.

☆ Many times during the Civil War, both sides would call a truce either at the end of the day or the end of the battle so they could collect their dead and wounded.

☆ Louisa May Alcott would write the novel *Little Women* after the war.

☆ William Black was 12 years old when an exploding shell shattered his left arm and shoulder. He may have been the youngest soldier wounded in the Civil War.

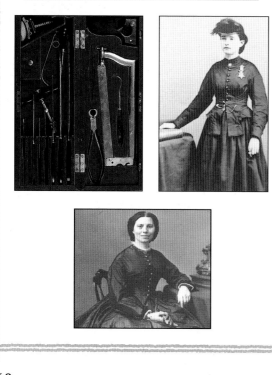

Of all the tragedies in the Civil War, perhaps the greatest was the primitive health care given to the wounded. Doctors knew almost nothing about germs. Antibiotics and other life-saving drugs didn't exist. To make matters worse, thanks to advances in weaponry, doctors found themselves treating by the thousands the worst wounds inflicted in the history of warfare. Rifles and muskets fired a lead bullet, called a "minié ball," that did terrible damage to the body. Because the minié ball was made of soft lead and was hollow, when it hit an arm or a leg bone, the bone shattered. To save the wounded soldier's life, the doctor had to amputate the limb. Doctors would use chloroform or ether to put the soldier to sleep. If the supply of anesthetics ran out, doctors tried to get the soldier drunk on whiskey. Sometimes, however, the only thing the soldier had to ease the pain was a bullet to bite on. The surgeon would then use a saw, still covered in blood from a previous amputation, to cut the limb as quickly as possible. The severed limb was tossed aside, the wound stitched shut, the soldier carried away, and another one brought in so the process could be repeated.

The United States Sanitary Commission was a large and powerful voluntary organization that took over most of the care of the wounded. Dorothea Dix, the superintendent of female nurses, worked with the commission to recruit nurses. Clara Barton became a one-woman soldiers'-aid society. Another remarkable nurse was Mary Ann Bickerdyke, a large, strong, maternal woman. Enlisted men fondly named her "Mother Bickerdyke."

The famous author Louisa May Alcott had been a nurse for only three days when wounded soldiers from the Battle of Fredericksburg arrived. She later wrote, "The sight of several stretchers each with its legless, armless, or desperately wounded occupant, entering my ward, admonished me that I was there to work, not to wonder or weep; so I corked up my feelings, and returned to the path of duty."

Many times, the only thing the doctors or nurses could do was help soldiers write a final letter home. One such soldier was Confederate J. R. Montgomery, who dictated: "My dear father, this is my last letter to you. I've been struck by a piece of shell. . . . I know that death is inevitable. I will die far from home, but I have friends here who are kind to me. May we meet again in heaven."

Top left: A Union army surgeon's amputation kit. *Top right:* Dr. Mary Walker wearing her Medal of Honor. *Bottom:* Clara Barton. *Opposite:* Wounded soldiers, some of them amputees, resting in the shade.

QUICK FACTS

★ Gen. Thomas became known as the "Rock of Chickamauga" for his heroic stand.

★ The Battle of Chickamauga had the second-highest number of casualties in the war—34,624. The Union suffered 16,170 casualties, and the Confederates suffered 18,454.

★ Gen. Bragg and his chief subordinates did not like one another and often quarreled. In fact, sometimes Bragg's generals wouldn't obey his orders.

★ Gen. Rosecrans, whose nickname was "Old Rosy," was a very religious man and something of a perfectionist. Lincoln, however, believed he lacked the kind of aggressive spirit needed to win and told a friend that Rosecrans behaved "like a duck hit on the head."

Above: Union general George H. Thomas. *Opposite:* A detail of Henry J. Kellogg's painting, *Battle of Kelly's Field* (at Chickamauga).

President Lincoln was very frustrated with the progress of the Union army of the Cumberland in the western theater in the summer of 1863. No matter what Lincoln said or threatened to do, the army's commander, General William Rosecrans, gave all kinds of excuses for not attacking General Braxton Bragg's Army of Tennessee. In early September 1863, just as the president was about to replace him, Rosecrans finally went on the offensive. In a series of quick maneuvers, Rosecrans forced Bragg's army to retreat across Tennessee.

Rosecrans succeeded in capturing Chattanooga, Tennessee, an important railroad center and a gateway to the Confederate heartland of Georgia. Meanwhile, Bragg created a plan that, if successful, would cut Rosecrans off from his base at Chattanooga and isolate his troops in a remote valley, where they would be forced to surrender. Gen. Longstreet had been ordered to take about 15,000 men from the Army of Northern Virginia to reinforce Bragg. On September 19, 1863, early morning skirmishing at Chickamauga Creek in northwest Georgia soon exploded into an all-out battle. Hard fighting continued, with neither side gaining a decisive advantage.

During the Confederate assault on September 20, Rosecrans received word from a staff officer that there was a dangerous gap in his front line where the rebels were attacking. The staff officer was wrong. In the confusion of battle, he had failed to see that the Union troops had simply hidden themselves in some nearby woods. Rosecrans immediately ordered another division to move over and fill the gap. When the division did, it left a *real* gap in the Union line right in front of Longstreet's troops. Longstreet's men charged, but instead of encountering an enemy, they found a quarter-mile hole in the Union line!

Panic struck the Army of the Cumberland. Union troops, including Gen. Rosecrans, started fleeing back to Chattanooga. Union general George H. Thomas organized a last-ditch stand and managed to fight off Longstreet's repeated assaults before finally retreating to Chattanooga. Gen. Thomas had saved the Army of the Cumberland from destruction. But now at Chattanooga, the Union army was trapped and the Confederate army surrounded it.

At one point in the fighting, Confederate officer William Oates encountered a young rebel soldier who was crying and well behind the attacking troops. Oates later wrote: "I spoke to him and told him not to cry; that he had not yet been hurt and he might live through the battle. . . . He replied, 'Afraid . . . ! That ain't it. I am so . . . tired I can't keep up with my company.'"

CHATTANOOGA

Right: Union general William S. Rosecrans. *Bottom:* Confederate general Braxton Bragg. *Opposite:* A crude but effective bridge constructed by Union troops.

The Confederate troops quickly followed up on their costly victory at Chickamauga Creek and trapped the Army of the Cumberland at Chattanooga on September 23. They held the high ground around the city, including Lookout Mountain. But Gen. Bragg could not press his advantage. His biggest problem was not with the Union army, but with his own fellow generals. The bickering got so bad that President Jefferson Davis had to step in and straighten things out. Soon the Confederates had another problem. On October 16, President Lincoln made General Ulysses S. Grant the supreme commander of the Union armies in the west in the newly created Military Division of the Mississippi.

Grant placed Gen. Thomas in command of the Army of the Cumberland and ordered him to hold Chattanooga "at all hazard." In late November 1863, Grant ordered forces under generals William Tecumseh Sherman and Fighting Joe Hooker to attack Confederate defenses. Sherman's attack on Missionary Ridge bogged down, but Hooker's men managed to seize the summit of Lookout Mountain.

Before the Union troops could claim total victory, they had to take heavily fortified Missionary Ridge. Gen. Thomas's Army of the Cumberland was ordered to seize only the bottom line of defenses, stop, and wait for reinforcements. But these veterans felt they had to wipe off the shame of defeat that lingered after Chickamauga. They not only took their objective, but they also continued fighting. They furiously charged straight up the slope. Grant and his generals were shocked at what they saw. They thought the attackers would be annihilated. Grant said darkly that if the assault failed, someone would pay dearly for it. But to the astonishment of everyone, Thomas's men successfully stormed the defenses and took Missionary Ridge. The Battle of Chattanooga had lasted from November 23–25. The way to Atlanta and the Confederate heartland was partially open to the Union forces.

After the second day of battle, a soldier in the 46th Ohio looked down at the body of a Confederate soldier lying on Missionary Ridge. The Yankee wrote: "He was not over 15 years of age, and very slender of size. He was clothed in a cotton suit, and was barefooted—barefooted, on that cold and wet 24th of November. I examined his haversack. For a day's ration there was a handful of black beans, a few pieces of sorghum and a half dozen roasted acorns. That was an infinitely poor outfit for marching and fighting, but that Tennessee Confederate had made it answer his purpose."

Above: A *Harper's Weekly* illustration of the New York draft riots showing rioters attacking the Colored Orphan Asylum. *Opposite:* A detail of Lilly Martin Spencer's painting, *War Spirit at Home (Celebrating the Victory at Vicksburg),* shows children playing soldier while their mother anxiously reads the news reports about the latest battle.

I am crying, because I have only seven sons left to fight the Yankees," Peggy Williams Patton of Virginia said proudly after she received word that her son Tazewell had been killed at Gettysburg. In 1861, such statements were common. But by 1863, not many people on the home front in the North or the South said such things. The dream of a short war had turned into a nightmare without an end in sight. Scott's Anaconda Plan blockade was hurting the South; shortages in everything, even food and clothing, were common. Many people were horrified by the number of soldiers who had been killed or crippled.

Married soldiers were in a difficult situation. Social Security, Aid for Dependent Children, and other modern government-sponsored programs did not exist in the 1860s. If a husband or father died or was crippled in battle, the surviving family faced real hardship. One Southern woman wrote to her soldier husband: "What do I care for patriotism? My husband is my country. What is country to me if he be killed?"

Many people in the South began to feel that the war had become "a rich man's war and a poor man's fight." They resented the fact that many rich, slave-owning plantation owners were still living at home while nonslave-owning men were in the army. By 1863, antiwar protests began to appear in both the Union and the Confederacy. Some were peaceful demonstrations; others were riots that left people killed or injured. On April 2, 1863, hungry citizens in Richmond, angry about the shortages of food in the city, staged the Richmond Bread Riot, demanding, "Bread! Bread! Our children are starving while the rich roll in wealth." The North suffered from popular unrest too. The United States suffered its worst riot in history when working-class men in New York City who hated the draft and who were worried about their jobs and futures went on a four-day rampage in July 1863. When the New York City Draft Riots ended, 105 people were dead.

Yet, even though some people in the North were getting weary of the war, most soldiers in the Union still felt the way an intensely Unionist Missouri officer did, who wrote in 1864, "*We must succeed. If not this year, why then the next, or the next. And if it takes ten years, why then ten years it must be, for we never can give up.*"

Lincoln's reelection in 1864 was an important turning point in the war. He had promised that he would fight the war to the finish and that he would accept only one result: total victory. At the end of 1864, only the most rabid secessionists believed that the Confederacy would win.

QUICK FACTS

★ Robert E. Lee was the son of a general who served in the Revolutionary War. His wife, Mary Custis Lee, was the great-granddaughter of Martha Washington, George Washington's wife.

★ When the war began, Lee was 54 years old and Grant was 39 years old.

★ When Grant was appointed brigadier general, his father told him, "Be careful. You're a general now; it's a good job, don't lose it."

★ Grant had once been a slave owner.

★ After the end of the war, Lee applied for parole in July 1865 to restore his U.S. citizenship. But because of a bureaucratic error, he did not officially receive it until 1975.

★ Grant would later become president of the United States. Four other Union officers in the Civil War would also become presidents: Rutherford B. Hayes, James A. Garfield, Benjamin Harrison, and William McKinley.

Robert Edward Lee and Ulysses Simpson Grant were two of the greatest generals in the Civil War. Lee was the son of one of the most distinguished families in Virginia. His former commander, Gen. Winfield Scott, considered Lee the greatest general in the army. Lee had no love for secession or slavery. He loved the Union, but, like many people back then, he loved his home state more. When Virginia seceded, Lee resigned from the U.S. Army and joined the Confederate army.

Lee was a natural leader who was idolized by his troops. In virtually all the battles he fought, he was outnumbered. His strategic and tactical brilliance made him a hero to the South and a feared and admired foe to his enemies. After the war ended, he accepted the presidency of Washington College in Lexington, Virginia. After his death in 1870, the school was renamed Washington and Lee University. Grant recalled that after Lee had surrendered at the town of Appomattox Court House, Virginia, in 1865, "I felt . . . sad and depressed . . . at the downfall of a foe who had fought so long and valiantly, and had suffered so much for a cause, though that cause was, I believe, one of the worst for which a people ever fought."

The very different Ulysses S. Grant was a man of no reputation and little promise when the war started. Yet by the time it ended, he had risen to the rank of lieutenant general, commanding all the Union armies. In 1868, he was elected president of the United States.

Grant had an informal, common-sense manner that inspired respect and obedience from his men. Unlike so many other commanders, Grant rarely demanded reinforcements, rarely complained, and rarely quarreled with associates. He just went ahead and did his job with the men and material he had at hand.

In his first assignment in the war, Grant was ordered to attack a rebel camp. As he approached it, he found himself filled with anxiety. But he controlled his nervousness and carried out his orders. When he and his troops arrived at the site, they discovered that the rebels had left. Grant realized the enemy colonel "had been as much afraid of me as I had been of him. This was a view of the question I had never taken before; but it was one I never forgot. . . . The lesson was valuable."

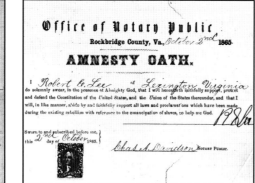

Above left: Abraham Lincoln's April 7, 1865 telegram tells Ulysses S. Grant to "let the thing be pressed" and to push Lee to surrender. *Above right:* The amnesty oath in which Gen. Lee pledges his support to the Union on October 2, 1865.

Opposite left: Union general Ulysses S. Grant. *Opposite right:* Confederate general Robert E. Lee.

QUICK FACTS

★ Gen. James Longstreet was accidentally shot by his own men during the Battle of the Wilderness. Unlike Stonewall Jackson, Longstreet survived.

★ The shooting was so intense at one point during the Battle of Spotsylvania that an oak tree nearly 2 feet thick behind the Southern lines was cut down by minié balls.

★ At Spotsylvania, the outnumbered Confederate army relied on field fortifications. They dug trenches and piled dirt in front and bolstered them with logs. These kinds of trenches became common for the remainder of the war.

Above: Gen. Grant (seated second from left in the pew in front of the two trees) checking a map during the Wilderness Campaign. *Opposite:* African Americans collecting the bones of soldiers killed in battle for burial.

When the war in Virginia resumed in the spring of 1864, George Meade still commanded the Army of the Potomac. But Grant, promoted to lieutenant general, traveled with Meade and made all the important decisions. For the first time in the war, Grant and Lee would be opponents on the same battlefield.

The first battle in Grant's Wilderness Campaign started on May 5 in "the Wilderness," a thick patch of woods near Chancellorsville, Virginia. The fighting was some of the most terrible in the war. Fires broke out among the trees, and the smoke got so thick that men couldn't see. That night, troops tried to rescue soldiers from the fire. One Union soldier later wrote: "Using my musket for a crutch, I began to pull away the burning brushwood, and got some of them out. One of the wounded Johnnies [rebels] . . . began to help. . . . We were trying to rescue a young fellow in gray. The fire was all around him. The last I saw of that fellow was his face . . . his eyes were big and blue . . . I heard him scream, 'O Mother! O, God!' It left me trembling all over like a leaf."

At one point, a brigadier general rushed up and urged Grant to retreat because of what he thought Lee was going to do next. "I am heartily tired of hearing what Lee is going to do," Grant angrily told the brigadier. "Some of you always seem to think he is suddenly going to turn a double somersault, and land on our rear and on both our flanks at the same time. . . . Try to think what we are going to do ourselves, instead of what Lee is going to do."

Grant tried to get past Lee and move south, but Lee blocked his way at the nearby town of Spotsylvania Court House and started building defenses. In the past, the Army of the Potomac would stop and rest after a big battle, giving the Army of Northern Virginia a chance to recover. But Grant refused to stop. The Battle of Spotsylvania began less than two days after the Battle of the Wilderness ended and lasted for over a week. At a place called the "Bloody Angle," soldiers on both sides leaped on the walls built by the defenders and fired down at the enemy with bayoneted rifles handed up from comrades below. Then they would hurl each empty gun like a spear before firing the next one. They did this until they were shot down or bayoneted themselves. The fighting—some of it hand-to-hand—continued until Lee ordered his men to retreat. Worse was to come in the battle at Cold Harbor.

QUICK FACTS

★ A Confederate survivor said of the battle-field, "The dead covered more than five acres of ground about as thickly as they could be laid."

★ After a month of combat, the Army of the Potomac had suffered 50,000 casualties, or 41 percent of its original strength. The Army of Northern Virginia had suffered 32,000 casualties, or 46 percent of its original strength.

★ "Lead mine" was the slang expression for a dead or badly wounded soldier who had been hit by a lot of bullets.

rant had lost about 38,000 men in the Wilderness Campaign. His predecessors would have all retreated. But Grant refused to back off. His goal was the Army of Northern Virginia and, beyond that, Richmond. Grant ordered his men to advance. His men were tired, but he knew Lee's soldiers were exhausted too. If he could outflank Lee, then the way to Richmond—and victory—would be his. Grant was hoping to reach the important crossroads town of Cold Harbor. But Lee got there first, just hours before Grant's men. The Army of Northern Virginia frantically began building defenses for the all-out battle that would occur.

The Army of the Potomac attacked on June 1, 1864. After two days of hard fighting, Grant could see no progress. Frustrated, he ordered a tremendous assault on June 3, at 4:30 A.M. His troops were slaughtered. Within an hour over 7,000 Union soldiers were shot down and the attack ended.

For three more days, the two armies warily faced each other, neither side requesting a truce to retrieve the wounded lying on the bloody ground that separated them. When litter bearers—men who carried wounded on stretchers—were finally allowed onto the battlefield, only two men were found still alive.

After the Battles of the Wilderness, Spotsylvania, and Cold Harbor, Gen. Meade said, "Grant has had his eyes opened and is willing to admit now that Virginia and Lee's army are not Tennessee and Bragg's army."

Though Grant would later regret the decisions he made at Cold Harbor, he did not change his strategy. He would continue to keep the pressure on Lee—this time at a town called Petersburg.

The ensuing campaign was seven weeks of nonstop marching and fighting. The stress on the men was incredible. Union captain Oliver Wendell Holmes Jr., wounded three times in the previous three years, wrote, "I tell you many a man has gone crazy since this campaign began from the terrible pressure on mind & body."

Above: A camp cook prepares a meal for men in the Army of the Potomac. *Opposite:* Gilbert Gaul's painting, *Battery H at Cold Harbor, Virginia.*

Above: Union general William T. Sherman.
Opposite: A lithograph of F. Darley's *William T. Sherman's March to the Sea.*

As general in chief, Grant was responsible for coordinating the movements of all the Union armies: Nathaniel Banks's Army of the Gulf in Louisiana, William Sherman's Army of Georgia located near Chattanooga, Franz Sigel's forces in West Virginia and the Shenandoah Valley, George Meade's Army of the Potomac, and Benjamin Butler's Army of the James on the Virginia peninsula. Grant's overall strategy was to have all his armies attack at the same time. This would keep the Confederate armies from reinforcing one another.

In the spring of 1864, Grant ordered Gen. Sherman to capture the Confederacy's major rail and supply center: Atlanta. Confederate general Joseph Johnston knew that his 62,000 men could not stop Sherman's army of 100,000. He also knew that the North was getting tired of the war. If he could somehow keep Sherman away from Atlanta until after the November elections, he reasoned, people would vote for politicians who would sign a peace treaty. Johnston's strategy was to make sure that his army avoided the all-out battle Sherman wanted for as long as possible. Johnston was successful, and Sherman grew frustrated. Unfortunately, President Davis thought Johnston was afraid to fight, so he replaced him with General John B. Hood.

On July 20, Hood ordered his army to attack. The Confederates fought bravely. But as Johnston knew, there just weren't enough of them and they retreated behind the trenches around Atlanta. On July 22, Sherman then laid siege to the city. With the situation getting more and more hopeless, Hood's army managed to escape just before Sherman completely surrounded the city at the end of August. Sherman ordered the civilian population expelled from the city, telling Atlanta's mayor: "War is cruelty. . . . [W]e are not only fighting hostile armies, but a hostile people, and must make old and young, rich and poor, feel the hard hand of war."

On September 2, 1864, Gen. Sherman sent a telegraph message to Washington: ATLANTA IS OURS, AND FAIRLY WON. The way was now open for Sherman's March to the Sea. On November 15, when the march began, his men put the torch to Atlanta, leaving the city in flames.

Noble C. Williams, a young boy who survived the siege, remembered that, "Citizens constructed . . . bombproofs, which were holes dug in the earth eight or ten feet deep . . . covered overhead with heavy beams which contained a covering of boards . . . and then covered with earth from three to five feet deep. The entrance . . . was dug out in the shape of the letter L" (to prevent shell fragments from entering).

QUICK FACTS

★ Sherman took 62,000 men with him in his March to the Sea.

★ Sherman's army cut a swath of destruction 25 to 60 miles wide.

★ Because Sherman didn't keep any supply or communication lines, no one in the North knew exactly where he was until he reached Savannah.

★ Union troops would rip up the iron rails from Southern railroad beds and bend them almost double so they couldn't be reused. These bent rails were called "Sherman's neckties."

Top: A Southern refugee family fleeing from Sherman's troops. *Above:* A cartoon depicts Sherman stuffing the gift of Savannah into Lincoln's Christmas stocking.

Having taken Atlanta, Gen. Sherman had to decide what to do next. Should he search for and attack Gen. Hood's army, with its 40,000 men? Or should he divide the Confederacy by continuing his march through Georgia and capturing the important seaport of Savannah? At first, he ordered his army to try to catch Hood and his men. But that proved impossible. Hood had learned his lesson during the Battle of Atlanta. Now he was playing a cat-and-mouse game. Sherman realized that if he kept this up he would be doing exactly what Hood wanted and that chasing Hood across Georgia and Tennessee would only prolong the war.

Sherman decided to send part of his army up to Tennessee to keep an eye on Hood's army. The rest of his army would march to Savannah. When Robert E. Lee had invaded the North with his army in 1862 and 1863, he had ordered his men to respect private property and pay for what they needed, though his men didn't always obey him. Sherman's march through Georgia in 1864 was different. The only things Sherman's army would carry would be ammunition and clothing. For everything else they needed, Sherman told his men they were to live off the land. This meant that whenever the soldiers found a farm or a plantation that had food and firewood, they would take what they wanted. What the army didn't take, more often than not, it destroyed.

Dolly Sumner Burge, a young widow with a nine-year-old daughter, wrote in her diary on November 19, 1864, about the soldiers who stopped at her plantation near Covington, Georgia: "Like famished wolves they came, breaking locks and whatever is in the way. . . . [T]hus ended the passing of Sherman's army by my place, leaving me poorer by $38,000 than I was yesterday. . . . And a much stronger Rebel."

Sherman became the most hated man in the South. But Sherman didn't care what the people said. To General Henry W. Halleck, he wrote as he was getting ready to leave Atlanta, "If the people raise a howl against my barbarity and cruelty, I will answer that war is war and not popularity-seeking."

One soldier in Sherman's army wrote of the wide path of destruction that the army made: "There is no God in war. It is merciless, cruel, vindictive, un-Christian, savage, relentless. It is all that devils could wish for."

Sherman reached Savannah in December and offered the city to President Lincoln as a Christmas gift. The South paid heavily for Sherman's "gift." Sherman himself estimated that his army had caused 100 million dollars' worth of damage in Georgia.

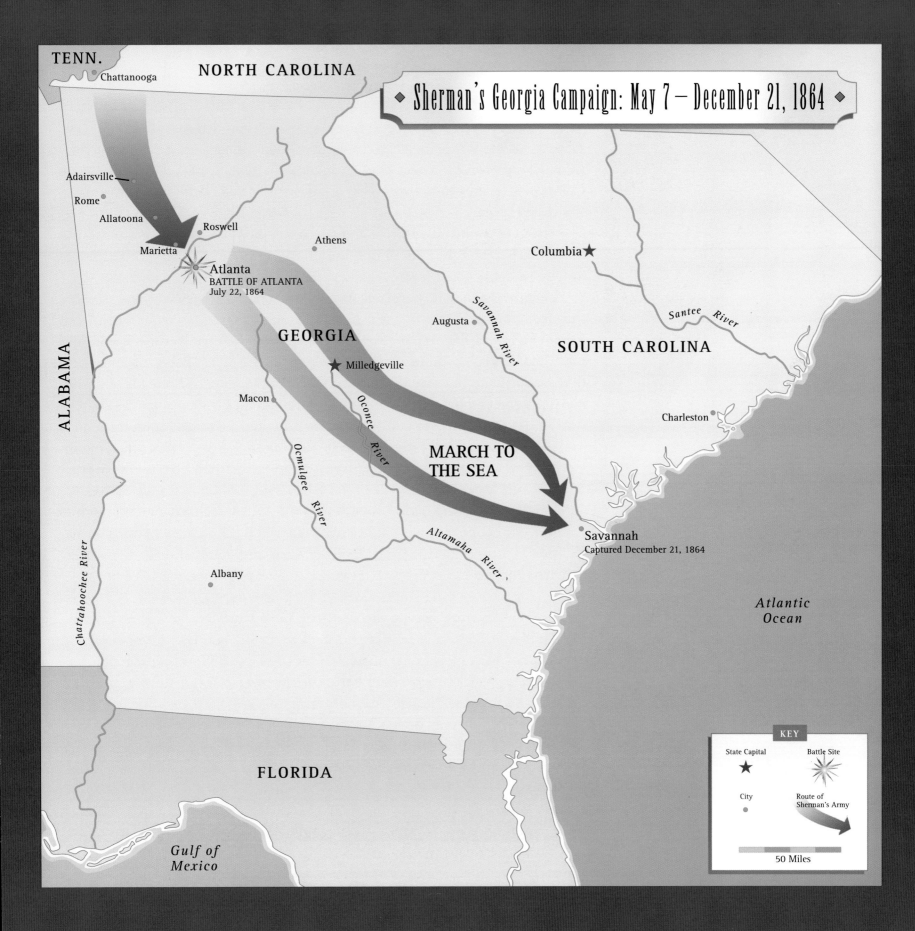

TENN.

NORTH CAROLINA

Chattanooga

Sherman's Georgia Campaign: May 7 — December 21, 1864

Adairsville

Rome

Allatoona

Roswell

Athens

Columbia ★

Marietta

Atlanta
BATTLE OF ATLANTA
July 22, 1864

GEORGIA

Augusta

Savannah River

SOUTH CAROLINA

Santee River

ALABAMA

★ Milledgeville

Macon

Oconee River

MARCH TO
THE SEA

Charleston

Ocmulgee River

Savannah
Captured December 21, 1864

Altamaha River

Albany

Atlantic
Ocean

Chattahoochee River

FLORIDA

KEY

State Capital

Battle Site

City

Route of
Sherman's Army

Gulf of
Mexico

50 Miles

THE BATTLE OF MOBILE BAY

After New Orleans was captured by the Union, Mobile, Alabama, was the most important port in the Confederacy. The entrance to Mobile Bay was guarded by three large forts. The approaches to the bay were filled with deadly torpedoes (mines), and a Confederate fleet including the giant ironclad CSS *Tennessee* guarded the port. On the morning of August 5, 1864, Adm. David Farragut, who had captured New Orleans, took his fleet of fourteen wooden ships and four ironclad monitors into the dangerous channel. If he could capture the forts that guarded this three-mile-long passage, he could cut off the port of Mobile at the opposite end of the bay, twenty miles away.

A terrific battle between forts and ships erupted. The smoke was so thick that Adm. Farragut had to climb high up a mast of his flagship, *Hartford*, just to see what was happening. *Tecumseh*, the lead monitor, hit a torpedo and sank. The next ship in line paused. Seeing this, Farragut shouted a command that made him a legend: "Damn the torpedoes! Full speed ahead!" By mid-morning, the Confederate fleet had been routed and the entrance to the bay was in Union hands. The Confederacy now had only one important port left: Wilmington, North Carolina.

It was common for young boys, ages ten to fifteen, to serve on warships in the nineteenth century. They were called "powder monkeys." Small, quick, and agile, these boys would scamper like monkeys across slippery decks that were filled with obstacles. They would go from cannon to cannon, bringing gunpowder, shot, or whatever else the gunnery crew needed.

The decks of the ships were terrible places during a battle. As John C. Kinney, an army signal officer on the USS *Hartford*, later wrote, during the battle, "a deadly rain of shot and shell was falling on [the *Hartford*], and her men were being cut down by scores, unable to make reply. The sight on deck was sickening beyond the power of words to portray. Shot after shot came through the side, mowing down the men, deluging the decks with blood, and scattering mangled fragments of humanity so thickly that it was difficult to stand on the deck, so slippery was it."

Left: One of the many boys who served on ships as powder monkeys—boys who carried ammunition and supplies to gun crews. *Opposite:* A detail of Julian O. Davidson's painting *Battle of Mobile Bay.*

Above: An "armored" cannon on a specially designed railroad car. *Opposite:* A section of the elaborate fortifications outside Petersburg.

The last great campaign of the war began on June 15, 1864. Petersburg, Virginia, was a communications center about twenty miles south of Richmond. Grant believed that if he could capture it, he could isolate the Confederate capital the same way he did Vicksburg the previous year. It was a good plan, and it almost worked. For one of the very few times during the war, Lee was surprised. He had only 3,000 men at Petersburg when 16,000 Union troops led by General W. F. "Baldy" Smith attacked. However, Smith's men were tired, and they had vivid memories of the recent slaughter at Cold Harbor. When reinforcements arrived to help the desperately fighting Confederates, Smith ordered his men to fall back and build defensive trenches to protect themselves.

The Battle of Petersburg turned into a siege that lasted almost ten months. Early on, Union soldiers convinced Gen. Burnside that they could blow a wide hole in the Confederate defenses by digging a tunnel under the rebel lines and exploding a mine. The Battle of the Crater took place on July 30, 1864. The explosive-packed tunnel blew a huge hole in the Confederate lines. Witness Union sergeant Thomas Bowen wrote: "In theory, the plan was rather ingenious. . . . The explosion, which could be heard for miles, sent Rebel soldiers and debris over a hundred feet into the air. All that remained was a smoldering crater 250 feet across and more than three stories deep. . . . And then everything went wrong. Instead of running around the crater, Union troops charged directly into it. Without ladders, they found it impossible to scale the thirty-foot dirt walls. . . . Confederate soldiers . . . rushed to the crater's edge, and rained a steel blizzard of bullets down on the cornered men."

As the siege of Petersburg continued, Grant's strategy was to keep the pressure on Lee. Grant had more men than Lee did, and Lee found himself having to do too many things with too few troops. The Army of Northern Virginia was like a thin rubber band being stretched to the breaking point. In March 1865, Lee saw that if he stayed where he was, he would lose both his army and Richmond. But if he escaped south with his army, there was still a remote chance of Southern victory. On April 2, Lee telegraphed Jefferson Davis, advising the government to leave Richmond, which it did that night.

On April 4, Abraham Lincoln entered Richmond and sat behind the desk that Davis had abandoned just two days earlier. Finally, after four long years, the defiant capital of the Confederacy that had somehow always escaped capture was now under Union occupation.

QUICK FACTS

★ The value of a prisoner depended on his rank. Usually, a general was worth 60 privates, a major general worth 40 privates, and so on. Privates were exchanged 1 for 1. Approximately 200,000 soldiers were freed through such exchanges.

★ During the summer of 1864, more than 100 prisoners a day died in Andersonville. By the time the war ended, the camp had held a total of 45,000 prisoners; approximately 13,000 of them had died of disease, exposure, or malnutrition.

★ Henry Wirz, commandant of Andersonville, was the only Confederate officer in the Civil War to be tried and convicted for war crimes. He was hanged.

★ Andersonville's official name was Camp Sumter. It is now a national historic site that honors all prisoners of war.

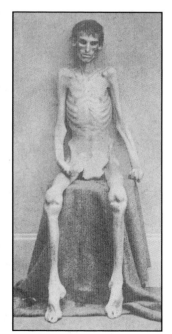

Left: A survivor from Andersonville.

When the Civil War started, neither side had a formal system for dealing with prisoners of war. At first, soldiers would usually be exchanged after a few weeks of being held in a temporary prisoner-of-war camp or in a local jailhouse. But as the war continued, exchanges stopped.

Some prisoner-of-war camps were worse than others. The worst camp in the North was Elmira Prison in New York. It was created in May 1864 and designed for 5,000 men; it held over 12,000 prisoners. Those who were not in the barracks had to live in tents—even in the bitter cold winter. Prisoners suffered from malnutrition and exposure. Reports of the terrible conditions reached the surgeon general, who ordered an investigation. But not even his report about the prisoners' suffering made any difference.

Andersonville, Georgia, was the location of the worst Confederate prisoner-of-war camp. Built in early 1864, Andersonville was a stockade camp of sixteen acres designed for 10,000 prisoners. It quickly became overcrowded. It was enlarged to twenty-six acres, and by August 1864, Andersonville held 33,000 prisoners-of-war. Conditions were horrific. There was no shelter from the hot sun. There was almost no food. The only drinking water came from a small stream that ran through the camp, and the stream was also used as a toilet.

Warren Lee Goss, a captured Union soldier, later described the sight that greeted him: "As we waited the great gates of the prison swung on their ponderous oaken hinges, and we were ushered into what seemed to us Hades itself. Strange skeleton men, in tattered, faded blue . . . gathered and crowded around us. . . . [T]he air of the prison was putrid; offal and filth covered the ground."

When word of the conditions in Andersonville reached the North, many politicians and newspaper editors demanded "eye for an eye" vengeance. "The enormity of the crime committed by the rebels," said Secretary of War Edwin Stanton, "cannot but fill with horror the civilized world. . . . There appears to have been a deliberate system of savage and barbarous treatment."

Despite these suspicions, the Confederacy did not have a deliberate policy of mistreating prisoners. The sad truth was that as the war started going against the South, *everyone* in the Confederacy suffered from a lack of food and supplies. Unfortunately, the people hit hardest were the people who were the most powerless: the Yankee soldiers in the prisoner-of-war camps.

Opposite: A view of Andersonville prison camp.

APPOMATTOX

Above: Thomas Nast's painting, *Peace in the Union,* shows Gen. Robert E. Lee shaking hands with Gen. Ulysses S. Grant at Appomattox. *Opposite:* A detail of Richard Norris Brooke's painting *Furling the Flag,* portrays the surrender of Confederate troops.

When Robert E. Lee was forced to evacuate Petersburg, he saw that his only chance to continue the war was to link his army with that of Joseph Johnston's in North Carolina. His Army of Northern Virginia tried to escape south. But at Appomattox Station, Union cavalry blocked the way. Out of supplies, outnumbered, and trapped, Lee recognized that further fighting was useless.

On Palm Sunday, April 9, 1865, Robert E. Lee dressed in his finest uniform and rode to the town of Appomattox Court House on his favorite horse, Traveller. Earlier that day Lee told an aide that he would rather "die a thousand deaths" than surrender. But he had no choice.

Adjutant W. Miller Owen, when he heard the news that the Army of Northern Virginia would surrender that day, recorded: "We had been thinking it might come to that, sooner or later; but when the shock came it was terrible. And was this to be the end of all our marching and fighting for the past four years? I could not keep back the tears that came to my eyes."

Lee waited for Grant at the home of Wilmer McLean. Grant hadn't had time to clean up when he received the news. Grant arrived in a dirty uniform, with mud on his boots.

Grant was generous with his surrender terms. He told Lee that after his officers and men surrendered, they would be paroled and ordered home. Once there, they would not "be disturbed by the United States authorities so long as they observe their paroles and the laws in force where they may reside." Lee asked that men who owned horses and mules be allowed to keep them as well. Grant agreed. Grant also authorized the distribution of food to Lee's half-starved army. Lee was grateful. He said, "[T]his will have the best possible effect on the men. It will be very gratifying and will do much toward conciliating our people." Lee signed the surrender document, shook hands with Grant, then left to tell his men the news.

Three days later, as the dejected Confederate troops approached the surrender site, Union major general Joshua L. Chamberlain gave a brief order, and a bugle call rang out. Instantly, the Union soldiers brought their weapons up into the position of carry arms, the salute of honor. Confederate general John Gordon stood at attention, turned to Chamberlain, dipped his sword in salute, and ordered his men to carry arms. Thus these enemies of many battles ended the war with a soldier's mutual salutation and farewell. Although there would be some minor skirmishes ahead, the Civil War was effectively over.

QUICK FACTS

★ It has been said of Wilmer McLean that the Civil War began in his front yard and ended in his parlor. In 1861, McLean had a home in Manassas during the 1st Battle of Manassas. His house was struck by artillery fire. Wanting to find a place where he thought the fighting would not reach him, he moved to Appomattox. It was in the parlor of his home that Lee surrendered to Grant.

★ Confederate Gen. Johnston surrendered his army to Gen. Sherman on April 26, 1865, near Durham Station, North Carolina.

★ The last battle of the Civil War was fought on May 13, 1865, at Palmito Ranch, Texas. The Confederates won.

★ As Grant recalled in his *Personal Memoirs,* "my own feelings . . . were sad and depressed. I felt like anything rather than rejoicing at the downfall of a foe who had fought so long and so valiantly, and had suffered so much."

QUICK FACTS

☆ Northerners who held positions of power in the South and used their power to make themselves, and their friends, rich were called "carpetbaggers" by Southerners. A carpetbag was a piece of luggage, like an overnight bag. These unscrupulous Northerners were in such a hurry to get to the South, the nickname implies, that they had only enough time to put clothes into one carpetbag. Most Northerners did not fit the negative stereotype.

☆ 3 amendments to the Constitution are known as the Reconstruction Amendments. The 13th Amendment, passed in 1865, abolished slavery. The 14th Amendment, passed in 1868, recognized racial equality. The 15th Amendment, passed in 1870, gave African Americans the right to vote.

☆ Robert E. Lee said, "I believe it to be the duty of everyone to unite in the restoration of the country and the reestablishment of peace and harmony."

Above: John Wilkes Booth. *Opposite:* A painting portrays the deceased Abraham Lincoln surrounded by mourners.

By the end of the war, the South was devastated. Its cities and farms were in ruins, its industry, way of life, and slavery were wiped out. Now came the greatest task of all—Reconstruction, the rebuilding and reuniting of the country. These post–Civil War years were a controversial time for the United States. Many people wanted to punish the South for the war. Others wanted to put the past behind them and work to rebuild the nation.

President Lincoln was thinking about what needed to be done, and he was relatively lenient in his thoughts on the South. Even before the war was over, Lincoln had announced his views on Reconstruction in his second inaugural address March 4, 1865: "With malice toward none; with charity for all; with firmness in the right, as God gives us to see the right, let us strive on to finish the work we are in; to bind up the nation's wounds; to care for him who shall have borne the battle, and for his widow, and his orphan—to do all which may achieve and cherish a just, and a lasting peace, among ourselves, and with all nations." It was a message both generous and merciful. Specifically, Lincoln suggested pardons for high-ranking Southern officers who pledged support to the Union. He also declared that if 10 percent of the voters registered in a rebel state took the loyalty oath, then this group of voters could form a new state government that would be recognized by the presidency.

But Lincoln never got the chance to see his vision materialize. Less than a week after Lee's surrender at Appomattox, on the evening of Good Friday, April 14, 1865, John Wilkes Booth, an actor who loved the Confederacy and hated Lincoln, entered the presidential box at Ford's Theatre and shot President Abraham Lincoln. Lincoln died the next day.

Booth escaped but was found two weeks later, on April 26, in a barn near Bowling Green, Virginia. The barn was set on fire, and Booth was shot to death trying to escape. Several hundred people were arrested on suspicion of conspiracy, but only four people were executed as accomplices in Lincoln's assassination.

Mrs. Elizabeth Keckley, the African-American dressmaker to Mary Todd Lincoln and a good friend, visited the president's body as it lay in state. She wrote, "No common mortal had died. The Moses of my people had fallen in the hour of triumph." At Lincoln's bedside when the president died, U.S. Secretary of War Stanton offered his own words of tribute: "Now, he belongs to the ages."

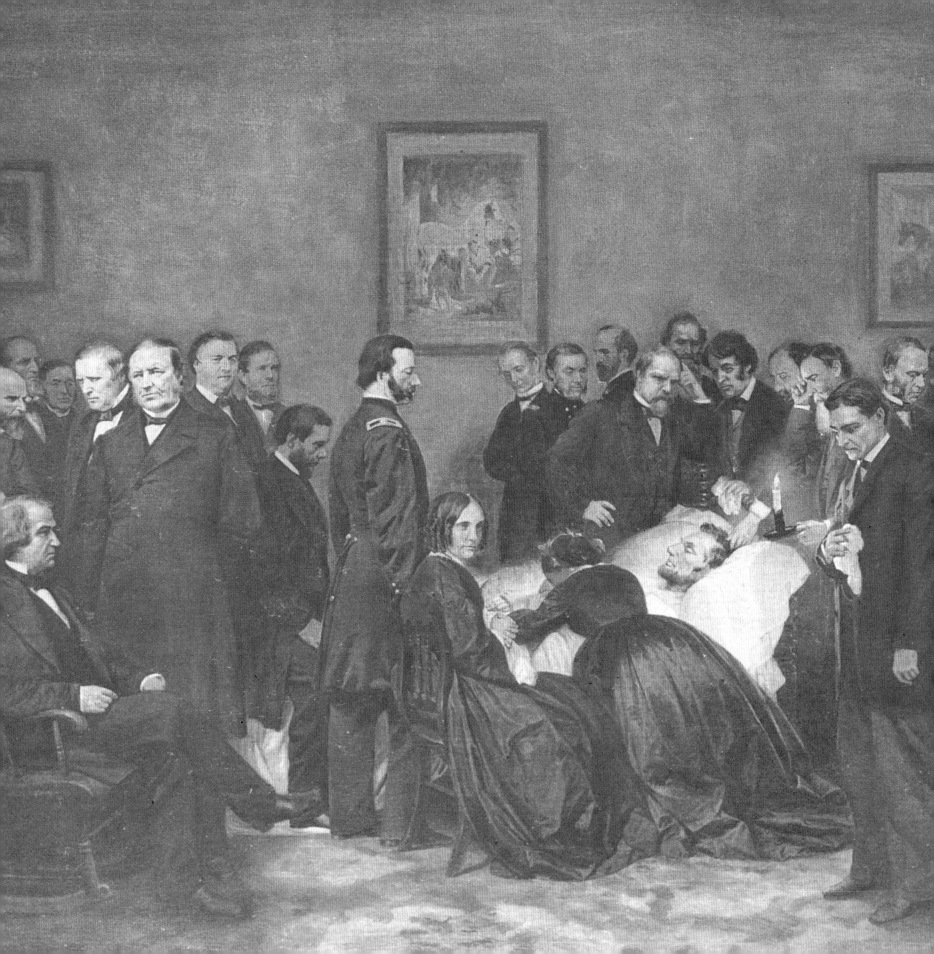

Above: An engraving of a carpetbagger.

Above: On the fiftieth anniversary of the Battle of Gettysburg, Confederate and Union veterans of Pickett's Charge shake hands.

Although Lincoln had never been popular in the South, seventeen-year-old Emma LeConte from Columbia, South Carolina, was among the more radical group of people who cheered the news. She wrote: "Hurrah! Old Abe has been assassinated! It may be abstractly wrong to be so jubilant, but I just can't help it. . . . This blow to our enemies comes like a gleam of light."

Lincoln's vice president, Andrew Johnson, became the new president, and he announced the official end of the Civil War on May 10, 1865. Unfortunately, he did not have Lincoln's diplomatic skills. Lincoln was a strong man who knew how to get people—even people who despised one another—to work together. The United States had lost the man who could heal the many emotional and physical scars left by the war.

President Johnson called for a policy of restoration, not Reconstruction, that was so generous that most of the Southern states voted back into office men who had held the same position in the Confederacy. Additionally, the Southern states passed Black Codes—harsh laws designed to reduce the freedmen to a status of near slavery. This infuriated the U.S. Congress, who took control of Reconstruction and pursued a stricter program.

Some good things were done during Reconstruction, such as passing important constitutional amendments abolishing slavery, granting African Americans citizenship, and giving them the right to vote. Congress created an agency called the Freedmen's Bureau. It gave food, clothing, medical assistance, and other kinds of help to newly freed slaves. Its most famous promise was that every freedman would receive from it 40 acres and a mule, though it did not fulfill that pledge.

When Reconstruction officially ended in 1877, many white Southerners still held their pre-war beliefs about African Americans. Even though the Black Codes were eventually revoked, white Southerners contrived to oppress former slaves. They did this by denying them the right to vote and by enforcing Jim Crow laws, which mandated unequal public facilities. This segregation reduced African Americans to second-class citizens. It was not until the Civil Rights movement in the 1960s that the Jim Crow laws were finally abolished.

It has been more than 120 years since Reconstruction officially ended. But the work to achieve harmony between the North and the South, as well as in race relations, continues. The economy of the South is now energetic and diverse, but it took almost a century for it to recover. Laws and legislation have been enacted to promote equality, but there's still more to be done before we achieve that goal. Yet we remain one nation, indivisible, with liberty and justice for all.

Opposite: African-American children in the ruins of Charleston, South Carolina.

GLOSSARY

Abolition—The act of eliminating slavery.

Abolitionist—Someone who believes in eliminating slavery.

Ambassador—The highest-ranking diplomatic representative of one country who is sent to another country.

Ammunition—Projectiles that are fired from weapons such as pistols, rifles, muskets, and cannons. These include bullets, cannon shells, and rockets.

Anarchy—The absence of any form of governmental authority.

Anesthesia—A drug that causes a loss of sensation, especially pain, with or without the loss of consciousness.

Annihilate—To destroy completely.

Arsenal—A place used to make and store weapons and ammunition.

Artillery—Weapons, such as cannons and mortars, that discharge ammunition.

Assassination—The murder of a public official or an important individual.

Assault—A military attack upon fortified enemy forces.

Barracks—A group of buildings used to house soldiers.

Battery—In the military, a grouping of cannons or mortars under a commander or in a warship.

Bayonet—A knife attached to the muzzle end of a rifle and used in close combat.

Blackguard—A rude person.

Blockade—The isolation of a region by a warring nation to prevent anyone or anything from going in or out.

Bombardment—An attack with artillery, such as cannon shots and shells or bombs.

Border states—A name applied to slave states, such as Maryland, Delaware, Kentucky, and Missouri, that either remained in the Union or were neutral and bordered upon the Northern states.

Breastworks—Temporary, hastily constructed low barriers used to protect soldiers.

Brethren—An old-fashioned word for "brothers."

Brigade—A large unit comprising two or more regiments and commanded by a brigadier general.

Brigadier—An officer of the army, usually a general, who commands a brigade.

Broadside—The simultaneous firing of all the cannons on one side of a warship.

Cabinet—A group of advisers to the president.

Campaign—A series of military operations undertaken to achieve a specific goal in a war.

Carpetbagger—A slang term for a Northerner who held a government position or who sought financial gain in the South after the Civil War.

Cavalry—Combat troops mounted on horses.

Chloroform—A colorless, volatile liquid used as an anesthetic in surgical operations.

Civilian—Any person who is not in the military.

Commemorate—To honor individuals or an event with a ceremony.

Commission—An official document assigning officer rank (lieutenant or higher in the army, ensign or higher in the navy) to a person in the military.

Conciliate—To become friendly or to appease.

Confederacy—An alliance between two or more people, groups, states, or nations in support of a common belief or goal.

Confederate—A person in a united group that has a common goal; in the Civil War, it usually referred to a citizen of the Confederate States of America.

Conspiracy—The secret planning of an unlawful or wrongful action by a group of individuals.

Constitution—A system of written fundamental laws and established institutions used to govern a country or state.

Contraband—During the Civil War, a slave who fled across or was smuggled behind the Union lines.

Courier—A messenger.

Cyclorama—A large pictorial representation, usually of a battle or landscape, displayed on a circular wall.

Debasement—A reduction in quality or value.

Decree—An order issued by a person in authority, usually having the force of law.

Defensive—In the army, getting prepared for an attack by an enemy, usually by building walls and digging trenches in order to protect soldiers.

Demoralize—To weaken the spirit or courage of a person or a group of people.

Diplomacy—The act of conducting relations between two or more countries.

Diplomatic recognition—The official acknowledgment of a country's existence by another country.

Dixie—The nickname for Southern states.

Dred Scott decision—A Supreme Court decision that stated neither Congress nor a territorial legislature could prohibit slavery in territories.

Election—The selection by vote for individuals who want to occupy a public office such as the presidency.

Emancipation Proclamation—President Lincoln's official declaration that freed the slaves.

Enlistment—The process of enrolling into the military.

Ensign—A national flag displayed on a ship; also may refer to a low-ranking officer in the Navy.

Ether—A highly flammable liquid once used as an anesthetic.

Export—Merchandise, weapons, and other goods sold and shipped from one country to another.

Federal—During the Civil War, a supporter of the U.S. government; generally, anything belonging to the U.S. government.

Firearm—Any weapon that shoots a bullet; usually a pistol, a rifle, or a musket.

Flank—The right or left side of a military unit.

Fleet—A group of warships acting together as a unit and under one commander.

Fortification—Defenses, usually walls and trenches, constructed to add strength to an army's position.

Fugitive Slave Law—The act of Congress in 1850 that ordered the return of runaway slaves from any state to which they had fled.

Greenbacks—Official U.S. paper money, printed with green ink, that was introduced in 1862 and is still used today.

Halliard—Alternate spelling of the word "halyard," which is a rope used to raise or lower a sail or flag.

Haversack—A canvas bag, similar to a knapsack, worn over the shoulder.

Import—To bring goods from one country into another.

Inauguration—An official ceremony inducting an individual into office.

Income tax— Money a government collects from an individual's or a business's earnings to help finance government expenses.

Infantry—Soldiers trained and equipped to fight on foot.

Insignia—A badge of office, rank, or membership in a group.

Ironclad—A warship that is completely covered in iron.

Jim Crow Laws—The systematic practice of segregating and discriminating against African Americans. Named after a fictional character in a popular play written before the Civil War.

Lanyard—A short rope used either to tie things on a ship or to fire certain types of cannons.

Malnutrition—A weakened condition of the body caused by insufficient or poor food consumption.

Maneuver—A strategic or tactical military movement designed to obtain an advantage over an enemy.

Mascot—Any person, animal, or object adopted by a group as a symbol of good luck.

Medal of Honor—The highest military award in the United States.

Militia—An army of enlisted citizens that has no officially trained soldiers, as in the regular army; usually called on during an emergency.

Mine—An explosive device used to destroy enemy personnel, fortifications, or equipment; it is usually placed under the ground and detonated when an individual or an object depresses its triggering device.

Minié ball—A soft, cone-shaped lead bullet hollowed at its base.

Minstrel show—A variety show, popular in the United States in the nineteenth century, in which white performers, painting their faces black, would sing, dance, and tell jokes that mocked African Americans.

Miscreant—A villainous person.

Monitor—An ironclad warship with a low, flat deck and one or more revolving turrets, equipped with cannons.

Musket—A smoothbore, long-barreled weapon fired from the shoulder.

Neutral—Belonging to neither side or party.

Nomination—The act of proposing someone for election to office.

Offensive—An attack.

Oppress—To keep down by the cruel or unjust use of power or authority.

Parole—The release of a prisoner before his or her sentence has expired on the condition of continued good behavior.

Pilot—A person licensed to steer ships into or out of a harbor or through difficult waters; today, the term also refers to a person who navigates airplanes.

Pincer movement—A military action in which flank movements are simultaneously used to attack an enemy from two sides and cut it off from support or escape.

Placard—A poster, small card, or metal plaque.

Plantation—A large estate or farm on which crops such as cotton or tobacco are grown and harvested by workers who live on the estate. Before the Civil War, these workers were generally slaves.

Powder monkey—A boy in the Navy who delivers ammunition to gun crews.

Pontoon—A flat-bottomed boat used by the military to construct temporary bridges for the transport of troops, weapons, and supplies.

Proclamation—An official announcement.

Provisional—Temporary.

Provisions—A stock of food and other supplies assembled for future needs.

Radical—An individual who desires revolutionary, often violent, changes in a present situation or circumstance.

Rebel—One who opposes authority; during the Civil War, it referred to any individual serving in the Confederate military or a citizen of a Confederate state.

Reconstruction—The process of reorganizing and readmitting the Southern states that had seceded from the Union.

Recruiter—A person who enlists others into the military or naval service.

Reenactor—A person who recreates an event from the past.

Regiment—In the Civil War, a military unit generally of ten companies, usually commanded by a colonel.

Revolution—The overthrow of an existing government or institution and its replacement with another.

Rout—In military terms, the disorderly and panic-stricken retreat of defeated troops.

Secede—To break away or leave an organization; during the Civil War, the act of states choosing to leave the United States to form the Confederate States of America.

Secessionists—In the history of the United States, individuals who believed in and advocated the right of a state to withdraw from the United States.

Segregation—The separation of a race or group from the rest of society.

Sentry—An armed guard of a military camp whose duty is to give a warning of danger.

Shell—A hollow casing, containing powdered explosives, that is fired from a cannon.

Siege—The surrounding and blockading of a town or fortress by an army that wants to capture it.

Silver nitrate—A colorless chemical used in photography and as a medicine.

Slaughter—To kill in a violent manner, and often to kill a great number of people.

Slavery—The state of one person being the property of another.

Sorghum—Syrup made from grain obtained from a grass by the same name.

Stereotype—The often oversimplified and prejudiced representation of a group of people in a way that strips them of any individuality.

Stockade—A barrier of stakes driven into the ground, side by side, either for defense against attack or to keep prisoners in an enclosed location.

Subordinate—Under the power and authority of another.

Swath—A broad path of destruction.

Tactic—In the military, a method of maneuvering forces in combat.

Territory—A region of the United States that is not part of any state and is governed by a legislature that is organized by, but independent from, the United States government.

Tourniquet—Any device used to stop the flow of blood from a wound.

Traitor—Someone who betrays his country, cause, or friends.

Treaty—A formal agreement between two or more nations.

Trench—In the military, a ditch usually used by soldiers for protection.

Truce—The suspension of fighting.

Typhoid fever—A highly infectious disease transmitted by contaminated food or water.

Union—During the Civil War, states that did not secede from the United States of America.

Volley—The simultaneous discharge of a number of firearms or artillery.

Volunteer infantry—A group of individuals who enter into military service of their own free will and serve as foot soldiers under a commanding officer elected by the group.

Western theater—In the Civil War, the military campaigns that occurred west of the Appalachian Mountains.

Yankee—A Union soldier in the Civil War; also, anyone from the North.

BIBLIOGRAPHY

Beschloss, Michael, ed. *American Heritage Illustrated History of the Presidents*. New York: Crown Publishers, 2000.

Boatner, Mark M. III. *The Civil War Dictionary*. New York: Vintage Books, 1988.

Catton, Bruce. *This Hallowed Ground*. New York: Doubleday & Co., 1956.

Catton, Bruce, and James M. McPherson, eds. *The American Heritage New History of the Civil War*. New York: Viking Press, 1996.

Chambers, John Witeclay II, ed. *The Oxford Companion to American Military History*. New York: Oxford University Press, 1999.

Clinton, Catherine. *Civil War Stories*. Athens, Georgia: University of Georgia Press, 1998.

Davis, Jefferson. *The Rise and Fall of the Confederate Government*, with a foreword by James M. McPherson. 2 vols. New York: Da Capo Press, 1990.

Davis, William C. *Rebels & Yankees: The Battlefields of the Civil War*. London: Salamander Books, 1999.

———.*Rebels & Yankees: The Commanders of the Civil War*. London: Salamander Books, 1999.

———.*Rebels & Yankees: The Fighting Men of the Civil War*. London: Salamander Books, 1999.

Davis, William C., Brian C. Phanka, and Don Troiani. *Civil War Journal: The Legacies*. Nashville: Rutledge Hill Press, 1999.

Donald, David Herbert. *Lincoln*. New York: Touchstone, 1995.

Fletcher, William A. *Rebel Private: Front and Rear Memoirs of a Confederate Soldier*. New York: Meridian, 1997.

Freeman, Douglas Southall. *Lee's Lieutenants: A Study in Command*. 3 vols. New York: Charles Scribner's Sons, 1942–1944.

Gallman, J. Matthew. *The Civil War Chronicle*. Agincort Press, 2000.

Garrison, Webb. *Civil War Curiosities: Strange Stories, Oddities, Events, and Coincidences*. Nashville: Rutledge Hill Press, 1994.

———.*The Encyclopedia of Civil War Usage*. Nashville: Cumberland House, 2001.

Golay, Michael. *Generals of the Civil War*. Rowayton: Dove Tail Books, 1997.

Guelzo, Allen C. "Lincoln and the Abolitionists." *Wilson Quarterly*. Washington, D.C.: Autumn 2000.

Harwell, Richard B. *The Confederate Reader: How the South Saw the War*. New York: Dover Publications, 1989.

———.*The Union Reader: As the North Saw the War*. New York: Dover Publications, 1996.

Holland, Mary Gardner. *Our Army Nurses*. Roseville, MN: Edinborough Press, 1998.

Johnson, Thomas H., ed. *The Oxford Companion to American History*. New York: Oxford University Press, 1966.

Kelly, C. Brian. *Best Little Ironies, Oddities & Mysteries of the Civil War*. Nashville: Cumberland House, 2000.

Madden, David., ed. *Beyond the Battlefield*. New York: Touchstone, 2000.

McPherson, James M. *Battle Cry of Freedom*. New York: Oxford University Press, 1988.

——— *For Cause & Comrades*. New York: Oxford University Press, 1997.

——— *The Negro's Civil War*. New York: Ballantine Books, 1965.

Montross, Lynn. *War Through the Ages*. New York: Harper & Row, 1960.

Morgan, Sarah. *The Civil War Diary of a Southern Woman*. New York: Touchstone, 1992.

Murphy, Jim. *The Boys' War*. New York: Clarion Books, 1990.

Patton, Robert H. *The Pattons*. Washington, D.C.: Brassey's, 1994.

Phillips, Charles, and Alan Axelrod. *Portraits of the Civil War*. New York: Barnes & Noble, 1993.

Quarles, Benjamin. *Lincoln and the Negro*. New York: Da Capo Press, 1991.

Taylor, Susie King. *Reminiscences of My Life in Camp with the 33rd U.S. Colored Troops, Late 1st South Carolina Volunteers*. Boston: Susie King Taylor, 1902.

Vaughan, Donald. *The Everything Civil War Book*. Holbrook, MA: Adams Media, 2000.

Velazquez, Loreta Janeta. *The Woman in Battle: A Narrative of the Exploits, Adventures, and Travels of Madame Loreta Janeta Velazquez*, C. J. Worthington, ed. 1876. Reprint, New York: Arno Press, 1972.

Waugh, Charles G., and Martin H. Greenberg. *The Women's War in the South*. Nashville: Cumberland House, 1999.

Werner, Emmy E. *Reluctant Witnesses: Children's Voices from the Civil War*. Boulder, CO: Westview Press, 1998.

Wheeler, Richard. *Voices of the Civil War*. New York: Meridian, 1990.

Woodward, C. Vann, ed. *Mary Chesnut's Civil War*. New Haven, CT: Yale University Press, 1981.

Yates, Bernice-Marie. *Jeb Stuart Speaks: An Interview with Lee's Cavalryman*. Shippensburg, PA: White Mane Publishing Company, 1997.

CIVIL-WAR SITES ON THE WEB

Go to the Internet, type the keywords "American Civil War," and you'll get more than a million Web sites dedicated to this subject. From museums to memorabilia, from reenactment events to battlefield sites, the opportunities to learn about and experience the greatest conflict fought on American soil have never been more available. Below is an admittedly small list of Web site addresses of some of the more notable sites devoted to the American Civil War. They are listed in alphabetical order.

Andersonville National Historic Site
www.nps.gov/ande/

Antietam National Battlefield
www.nps.gov/anti/

Appomattox Court House National Historic Park
www.nps.gov/apco/

Chickamauga & Chattanooga National Military Park
www.nps.gov/chch/

Civil War Links
http://history.acusd.edu/gen/classes/civilwar/links174.html

Fort Donelson National Battlefield
www.nps.gov/fodo/

Fort Sumter National Monument
www.nps.gov/fosu/

Frederick Douglass National Historic Site
www.nps.gov/frdo/

Fredericksburg & Spotsylvania National Military Park
www.nps.gov/frsp/

Gettysburg National Military Park
www.nps.gov/gett/

Harpers Ferry National Historical Park
www.nps.gov/hafe

Index of Civil War Information
www.cwc.lsu.edu/civlink.htm

Kennesaw Mountain National Battlefield Park
www.nps.gov/kemo/

Library of Congress
www.loc.gov

Lincoln Home National Historic Site
www.nps.gov/liho/

Manassas National Battlefield Park
www.nps.gov/mana/

The Museum of the Confederacy
www.moc.org

The National Archives and Records Administration
www.nara.gov

Petersburg National Battlefield
www.nps.gov/pete/

Richmond National Battlefield Park
www.nps.gov/rich/

Shiloh National Military Park
www.nps.gov/shil/

Stones River National Battlefield
www.nps.gov/stri/

Ulysses S. Grant National Historic Site
www.nps.gov/ulsg/

U.S. Civil War Collections
www.umd.umich.edu/lib/sci/civilwar.html

Vicksburg National Military Park
www.nps.gov/vick/

INDEX

1854

MAY 30
Kansas-
Nebraska Act

1857

MARCH 6
Dred Scott
decision

1859

OCTOBER 16–18
John Brown's Raid,
Harpers Ferry,
Virginia

1860

NOVEMBER 6
Abraham
Lincoln elected
president

DECEMBER 20
South Carolina
secedes from the
Union

1861

JANUARY 9–26
Mississippi,
Florida, Alabama,
Georgia, and
Louisiana secede
from the Union

FEBRUARY 1
Texas convention
votes for
secession from
the Union

FEBRUARY 18
Jefferson Davis
inaugurated as
provisional
president of the
Confederacy

MARCH 4
Abraham
Lincoln
inaugurated as
president of the
United States

APRIL 12
Confederates
open fire on
Fort Sumter in
Charleston
Harbor, South
Carolina

APRIL 17
Virginia
convention
votes for
secession from
the Union

MAY 6
Arkansas
secedes from
the Union

MAY 6
Tennessee
legislature
passes secession
ordinances

1863

APRIL 16
Union launches
campaign to capture
Vicksburg, Mississippi

JANUARY 1
Lincoln signs
Emancipation
Proclamation

JULY 1–3
Battle of
Gettysburg,
Pennsylvania
(Union
victory)

MAY 1–4
Battle of
Chancellorsville,
Virginia
(Confederate
victory)

JULY 13–16
New York
City draft
riots

JULY 4
Vicksburg,
Mississippi,
surrenders to
the Union

SEPTEMBER 19–20
Battle of
Chickamauga, Georgia
(Confederate victory)

SEPTEMBER 9
Union troops
occupy
Chattanooga,
Tennessee

NOVEMBER 19
Lincoln's
Gettysburg
Address

SEPTEMBER 23
Confederate
troops begin siege
on Chattanooga,
Tennessee

NOVEMBER
23–25
Battle of
Chattanooga,
Tennessee
(Union victory)

1864

MAY 5–6
Battle of the
Wilderness,
Virginia (no
clear victory)

MAY 7
Sherman
begins
Atlanta
Campaign

MAY 8–19
Battle of
Spotsylvania
(Union
victory)

JUNE 1–3
Battle of
Cold Harbor,
Virginia
(Confederate
victory)

JUNE 15
Union begins
siege of
Petersburg,
Virginia
(Union
victory)

JULY 30
Battle of t
Crater, Virg
(Confedera
victory)

JULY 22
Battle of
Atlanta
(Union
victory)